PRICELESS DIAMOND

PRICELESS DIAMOND

A DIAMOND RING DARK ROMANCE

THE KIDNAPPED SERIES
BOOK 4

ALIX KEY

This is a work of fiction. Any references to historical events, real people, or real locales are used fictitiously. Other names, characters, places, and incidents are products of the author's imagination, and any resemblance to actual events or locales or persons, living or dead, is entirely coincidental.

Published by Diamond Freeport Press
P.O. Box 42133, Arlington, VA 22204

ISBN 978-1-95018-476-7

Discover other titles by Alix Key at www.alixkey.com

091625ak

ALSO BY ALIX KEY

Find a complete, up-to-date list of Alix's books at www.alixkey.com.

The Kidnapped Series

Diamond Solitaire

Rough Diamond

Conflict Diamond

Priceless Diamond

The Irish Mob Trilogy

Irish Brute

Irish Vice

Irish Reign

The Boston Mob Trilogy

Her Irish Savage

Her Irish Protector

Her Irish King

The Taming the Mob Princess Trilogy

Taken Enemy

Twisted Enemy

Tamed Enemy

The Sinful Mafia Series

Sinful Mafia Santa

Sinful Mafia Deception

Sinful Mafia Seduction

Sinful Mafia Salvation

WORD OF WARNING

***Priceless Diamond* is a dark romance.**

It contains hard-to-read scenes, graphic language, and explicit sexual content.

A complete list of potential triggers can be found at:

https://alixkey.com/books/kidnapped-series/

Please don't read this book if you are sensitive to any of those triggers. But if you believe in the redemptive power of love to overcome near-unimaginable trauma, then this is the book for you.

Welcome to the Diamond Ring.

THE KIDNAPPED SERIES, A RECAP

Have you read the first three books in the Kidnapped Series?

You can get started with *Diamond Solitaire*, by typing

https://alixkey.com/PB0US

into your phone or computer browser. And you can continue with *Rough Diamond*, by typing

https://alixkey.com/PB1US

into your phone or computer browser. Then you can wrap up by typing

https://alixkey.com/PB2US

into your phone or computer browser.

If you don't want to read them—or if it's been a while—

here's a quick summary of the Kidnapped Series so far (minus, of course, the spicy scenes!)

~

Alix Key and Travis "Trap" Prince enjoy a one-night stand where, against all odds, they bond on an emotional level, each healing a deep wound in the other. But when Alix returns home from the tryst, she is kidnapped.

She wakes to find that her desperate, addicted brother Leo sold her to drug kingpin Klaus Herzog. A sexual sadist, Klaus holds Alix as a slave for three years.

Trap spends that time searching for Alix and building his billionaire's tax haven, Diamond Freeport. Klaus becomes one of unknowing Trap's most important clients.

When Herzog brings Alix to a dinner party at the freeport (her first time out in public since she was enslaved), she seizes a steak knife and stabs him to death. Trap and his richest clients cover up all evidence of the death.

Trap and Alix then begin to rebuild their relationship, but that emotional connection is disrupted by blackmail. Klaus's brothers have video of the murder which they will release if Trap doesn't pay one billion dollars and provide a freeport warehouse for their illegal drug operations.

While Alix is tormented by guilt that she has put the freeport at risk, Trap attempts to gain the upper hand over the brothers. Ultimately, he hires mercenaries to attack their Long Island stronghold, but the raid fails and the video is released.

Hounded by paparazzi, Alix and Trap are investigated by the police for Klaus's murder. Trap's clients remain at risk of blackmail for their roles in the cover-up.

When Trap learns that the brothers will be at a Brooklyn sex club, he forges a plan to kill them, removing their threat to Alix and his clients. Alix follows Trap to the club, where she is forced to play a BDSM scene with the Herzogs. She suffers flashbacks and reverts to her slave mentality.

Trap rescues Alix, but she demands to be taken to Klaus's mansion. There, she begs Trap to abuse her the sadistic way Klaus did. Repulsed, Trap leaves.

While haunting the house, Alix discovers a stash of videos that show her servicing Klaus's powerful "special guests". Realizing she was exploited, she understands why Trap would not treat her in the way that she craved.

Alix and Trap reconcile, returning to the freeport with the videos. When Alix explores the computer files further, she discovers that her brother Leo is actually still alive…and he is working for the Herzog brothers.

1

ALIX

Some nightmares never die.

My hands shake as I stare at the photograph of the man who sold me into sexual slavery. Leo Key. My brother. My twin.

He's supposed to be dead. That's what one of the women said, one of the slaves who was tortured with me in Klaus Herzog's mansion in the Delaware woods.

"Princess?"

Trap stands in the doorway to his bedroom—*our* bedroom—holding an insulated mug filled with coffee. Given the look of concern on his face, I must have made some noise while I stared at the evidence I just found.

I shut the computer, as if folding down the screen is enough to push Leo out of my life. My hands are shaking. For some reason, I can picture my brother and me playing hide-and-seek in my grandmother's house. We must be five or six years old, and Leo just jumped out of Granny's closet, screaming bloody murder and making me cry.

"Princess?" Trap asks again. "What's going on?"

"Leo," I say, but my voice doesn't sound like my own. "Leo's alive."

Trap doesn't call me a liar. He doesn't question where I got my information. Instead, he crosses the room and forces my fingers around the mug. He tucks his hand under my elbow and guides me to sit on the side of the bed.

I stare at the coffee. It's easier to talk to a mug than to Trap—especially after having told him the truth last night, the entire truth, that I love him and can't imagine living my life without him.

Something tugs at me in the morning light. It costs too much to love me, even if Trap is a billionaire.

I killed a man in the most violent way possible. The police investigation into my crime is dragging Trap down too. His most loyal clients are on the hook because of me—targeted by my victim's brothers.

And now… With Leo still alive…

It's all too much. I'm dissolving. I'm melting into a ghost of the woman Trap once knew.

I force myself to piece together the facts I know, to tell them to the mug. "Back at Herzog's house… Lilyana, my best friend there… She said Leo was a… boyfriend to several of Herzog's women. He raped them, Trap. He brought them chocolates and colored pencils and they thought he was their friend, but he forced himself on them when they didn't have a choice."

"The whole place was fucked up," Trap says. He must think his words will make things better, but I see the cords tense in his wrists. The skin on his knuckles is tender and pink. He's punched walls and guards to tear down my nightmare, and I have no doubt he'd reduce Herzog to a pulp if I hadn't already killed my tormentor.

He'd destroy Leo for me.

But I'm still trying to make sense out of the files I just saw on the computer. "Lilyana was so certain," I say. "She said Leo owed Herzog. Leo promised me as payment of his debt. He told Herzog I was a virgin, and they agreed that three days with me would clear the ledger."

It's a good thing I'm still talking to the coffee, because Trap is straining beside me, barely biting back all the things he wants to say. He knows Leo was wrong. I wasn't a virgin. Leo lied *before* I spent the most magical night of my life here, with Trap, in this room, in the bed we're sitting on right now.

"I heard him," I say. "Leo. I heard him at Herzog's house." I don't know why I need to defend my brother, why I feel the urge to protect him even now. But twenty-six years of living with Leo burned pathways in my brain. He was my twin. I knew him.

He *is* my twin. I *know* him.

I force myself to finish my thought. I tell the coffee, "In Herzog's house. Even before I knew where I was, when I was in the Holding Room, and the drugs they gave me were first wearing off, I heard Leo begging. Pleading. He said, 'Please. I'm sorry. I'll do better. Please! Don't do this to her.'"

Trap's hand is gentle on mine, even though I can feel the tension in his fingertips. He takes the cup of coffee and puts it on the nightstand. With his other hand, he cups the curve of my jaw. He echoes Leo's unsuccessful plea. "Don't do this to yourself."

"I loved him!" I say, my voice breaking on the second word.

"I know." Trap wants to make everything right. But the truth is he doesn't know how. He *can't* know how.

I'm not sure I have the words to tell him, but I have to try. "We used to joke about sharing one brain," I say. "Leo and me. 'I need the brain for third period. I have an algebra test.'"

"Let it go, Princess," Trap says. His fingertips are gentle on my cheek, and I'm surprised to see they come away wet.

I dash the back of my hand against my face. I don't want to be crying. "He followed the rules. We both did, all the way through high school. Really bad things happened to us—Mom died, and Dad married Candace, and she moved in with her daughters so Leo had to sleep in the basement on that horrible creaky futon…"

"It was a long time ago," Trap says.

He's right. But he's wrong, too, because it feels like yesterday. The wounds of childhood and adolescence are deep, the heart-blood way too bright. "We stood up to them together. I watched Leo in *Twelve Angry Men* when Dad was too busy to go to a school play. Leo went to my choir concert. He brought me daisies! My favorite!"

Trap sighs. But he doesn't try to stop me. Not anymore.

"Leo and I got drunk together, the night of high school graduation. We stole a bottle of bourbon from the liquor cabinet and went to the park at the end of the street. Neither of us even liked bourbon, but Candace did, and we wanted to take something from her."

We drank until the world spun around us. Until I puked. Leo held my hair back and told me I would be okay, and I believed him.

"It wasn't until college that he started using. Adderall first, because his roommate said it would help. Then meth. And ecstasy. And Crash."

"It wasn't your fault." Trap tries again.

"I was supposed to be there for him. He was my *twin*." I don't realize I shouted the last word until the echoes push against my eardrums. "He was my twin," I repeat, whispering this time. "And when everyone walked away—Dad and all our family, all our friends… I was the only one who could help him. The only one who could save him."

"Leo could have saved himself." I know Trap's tone. It's the calm reasoning of a group leader at Al-Anon. It's the detached truth of a therapist. I've heard variations on those words dozens and dozens of times.

"He needed help," I say. I don't need to be defensive. Trap

loves me, no matter what mistakes I've made. But I hear the knife edge in my words. I feel the shame. The frustration. The helpless, heartless anger when Leo slipped again and again and again.

Eight trips to rehab. A week here. Two weeks there. Once, the last time, for two solid months.

I thought I could help him. I thought I could heal him.

I was wrong.

"I lost my family for Leo. I lost my friends. I lost my fiancé."

Trap snorts at that, like he just can't help himself. I know he thinks Jason Carter wasn't much of a loss.

Jason wasn't the man I thought he was. Our relationship wasn't the dream I believed. If Leo hadn't driven Jason off, I would have gotten married, would have followed my husband to some small university town in the Midwest, would have sacrificed my career for his.

I never would have had an orgasm. Not once. Not with Jason. Not even when I pleasured myself. I never would have *imagined* the toys stored in the bottom drawer of Trap's dresser, just across the room.

My cheeks heat, but that just gives me fuel to name Leo's worst sin. "I lost you."

Three years, I could have been with Trap.

Three years, I could have explored the knife-edge of pleasure and pain.

Three years, I could have learned the inner workings of Diamond Freeport, Trap's billionaire tax haven.

Three years, I could have become me. Become us.

"You didn't lose me," Trap says. "I'm still here."

"But all that time we could have had together…" My voice quivers because I'm nearly overwhelmed by the thought of everything I lived through during those long years. "Instead, I was a slave. I was raped over and over and over again. I killed Klaus Herzog, right here, in this house."

I can see Trap wants to stop me. He wants to interrupt. But

I hold up a hand, because this is my best chance to make him understand. My best chance to make clear exactly what I need and why I need it. "Because of me, because of Leo, we're waiting to see if the police will charge us with murder. Because of me, because of Leo, the tax authorities may shut down the freeport. Because of me, because of Leo, every member of the Diamond Ring, your best and richest clients, might be blackmailed by Klaus's brothers."

He's shaking his head. He doesn't want to accept that any of this is my fault. He doesn't want to agree.

But I know the truth. And I'm almost there. I've almost finished telling him what I need. "Bring him here."

"What?" He's confused. This isn't what he expected.

"Bring Leo to the freeport." I nod toward the computer on top of the dresser. "His address is in there. It's just in Philadelphia."

"Why the fuck would I want that piece of shit in my home?"

"*You* don't want him. But I do. Because once he's here, I'm going to kill him."

2

TRAP

A family of tourists stands outside Philadelphia's Mummer's Museum, oohing and aahing over the memories they're making for a lifetime. "Excuse me! Sir?" the mother says. "Could you take our picture?"

What's wrong with a fucking selfie?

I think it. I don't say it. I take their thousand-dollar phone and wonder what they'd do if I tore off down the alley with it. Instead, I tell them all to say cheese. I'm a goddamn upright citizen.

At least, that's what I hope to project before I slink into the Hare and Harp, a down-at-the-heels bar with mahogany walls, a long scarred counter, and a private office for the captain of Philadelphia's Irish mob. "He in?" I ask the bartender, who's polishing a glass like his life depends on it.

"Who's asking?"

"Trap Prince."

The barkeep scowls, but he taps out a text on the phone he

pulls from his apron pocket. Nice to know organized crime is keeping up with the times.

"You know where the office is?" the guy finally asks.

I don't bother answering. I just head down the hall, past a storage room and a steep set of stairs that lead to a basement where I suspect things happen that I'm better off knowing nothing about.

I knock twice on the door at the end of the corridor and wait for a shout—"Come in!"—before I turn the knob.

Braiden Kelly sits behind a desk that looks like it was salvaged from some ancient Irish ship. The front and sides are carved with harps and shamrocks and those tall buckled hats that leprechauns wear. A gooseneck lamp stands on top, highlighting a statue of St. Brigid and a fan of mass cards.

Kelly stands when I enter. I tolerate his handshake, snarling at the Beast inside my skull and clenching my other first around my cell phone for a quick five-count. Kelly waves to one of the two massive armchairs that crowd the rest of the office. I take the one angling toward the door, putting my back against the wall.

"My man Liam should've sent you back with a pint," Kelly says.

"He must have realized I'm not staying long."

Kelly probably figured that out on his own. Sure, Kelly's in the Diamond Ring, one of my top twelve clients at the freeport. But that doesn't mean I drop in on a regular basis to shoot the shit.

He rubs a hand over his face, and I wonder what I interrupted. The guy looks tired; there are spider lines of red around his blue eyes. He hasn't shaved in a week or more. Maybe that's because his beard drives women crazy. Or the made men of Philadelphia might have some sort of problem on their hands.

Not my fucking circus. Definitely not my goddamn monkeys.

"I need some help," I say.

His face twitches, just a raise of his eyebrows. "What sort of help?"

I glance around the office, wondering if I'd recognize surveillance equipment if I was staring right at it. I figure Kelly's got to sweep the joint on a regular basis. He might be able to buy protection from Philly cops, but the feds aren't as easy to keep on a payroll.

"Go on," he says. "The office is clean."

"I need some help picking up a guy. He's in a warehouse, down by the Navy Yard."

"Some help." His voice doesn't go up, but he's asking a question.

"He's employed by the Herzogs, Jonas and Ansel. The assholes who made that video public."

He doesn't have to ask which video. The footage of Alix killing Klaus Herzog has been front and center on local news for over three weeks. I told the Diamond Ring about it myself, at the same time I suggested they all take long vacations to countries without extradition treaties.

No one took me up on it. I chose the Diamond Ring well. Except for Klaus—and I'd been warned off him from the beginning. I let money outweigh my common sense, and I'll be paying off the debt for years.

Kelly sits back in his chair and purses his lips. He picks up an ivory-handled letter opener and taps the metal tip against the blotter on his desk. "You want to grab some low-level soldier? Not the top brass?"

I shrug. "I've got plans for those cocksuckers." Syringes filled with potassium chloride, if I have my way. Same drug prisons use to execute murderers and rapists. "This is a different beef."

Kelly's not impressed with my logic. "Sounds like this is more a job for Best's men."

He's talking about Sawyer Best, another member of the Diamond Ring. At my request, the mercenaries of Best's

Sawgrass Corporation went up against the Herzogs last month, and the operation was fucked up to the tune of eight men dead.

Not Best's fault. But reason enough for me to say, "They're not big on adding freelancers to the team."

"You want in on this yourself?"

I shrug. I don't *want* to do this. I'd rather be home with Alix, tying her to the bed and seeing how many ways I can make her come before midnight.

But this is what Alix asked for. This is what she needs. So, yeah. I want in on it myself. "It's personal," I tell Kelly.

"You know how to handle a gun?"

He doesn't mince words. That's another reason he's in the Ring. "I can get the job done."

"You've got a clean weapon? Or am I supplying one?"

He's asking if my gun's been used in a crime. My Sig Sauer was bought new. The only action it's seen has been at the gun range. "I've got my own."

He nods with a narrow-eyed look that I think is appreciation. "And this boyo you want picked up. What's he do for the brothers?"

"Near as I can tell, he's packing drugs. Meth. Heroin. Crash."

Kelly pinches the bridge of his nose before he meets my gaze. "Operation like that," he says. "It'll be well protected."

"My guy doesn't exactly have a union pushing for coffee breaks and overtime pay. There's a good chance they keep him chained up overnight. Might be easier to get him then."

"Or not. Business like that might sleep during the day."

I spread my hands to indicate I've got no horse in the fucking race. "With an address on hand, your men can take a look around. Figure out the best approach. I'll come back for the actual pick-up. You get first dibs on anything left lying around."

Drugs. I'm not bringing them into the freeport.

"Pick-up." He repeats my phrase. "Is that a polite way of saying we're dumping him in the river?"

Honestly, I'd be happy enough to put a bullet through Leo Key's brain. But that's not what I promised Alix.

"No. I meant what I said. Pick him up. Hood the asshole so he doesn't know where he's going. Get him to the freeport and I'll deal with him from there."

Kelly thinks for almost a minute before he nods. "We can do that."

"Got a timetable?"

"Give me a week to see what's what, whether we go in at night or during the day. Either way, we'll make a move Saturday next."

Eight days from now. Alix will have to live with the wait.

Neither of us believes in karma or any of that shit. I'm not worried about a stain on her soul—whatever the fuck that means—or on mine.

But Alix and her brother grew up close, and they got a hell of a lot closer when his using cut them off from the rest of the world. I learned that when I tried to find her three years ago. When I tracked down her family and that pussy she was going to marry.

This revenge shit is twisted.

I know the fucked-up things Herzog did to Alix. And there's no way in hell I'm going to judge her for anything she does to the cocksucker who put her there. But I plan on spending the next week convincing her to let me take care of him. Let her move on in peace.

Kelly's waiting. "Yeah," I say. "Next Saturday's good. And your price?"

He taps that letter opener again. The tip is sharp enough to take out an eye. "Sounds like you're giving me a chance to clean up a blight on the Philadelphia waterfront."

"I didn't come here for charity."

"Let's see how it plays out. If we pick up collateral goods, we'll call it even. Otherwise you'll owe me one. Deal?"

Collateral goods. Fuck, I'm tempted to pay Kelly extra to walk off with the Herzogs' drugs. Kick them where it really hurts. But I say, "Deal."

Kelly slides open one of the drawers in his desk and comes up with two shot glasses and a bottle of eighteen-year-old Jameson's. He pours with a heavy hand and passes one to me. "Slainte," he says.

I echo the toast. Neither of us tosses back the liquor. We're too fucking civilized for that. We sip like sophisticated motherfuckers.

"This boyo," he says after I acknowledge the superiority of the whiskey. "He have a name?"

"Key," I say. "Leo Key."

Kelly's not afraid to meet my gaze. "Like Alix."

"Yeah. Like Alix."

Kelly was there the night Alix sliced open Klaus Herzog's carotid and carved his dick into dog food. Now, he gives me a look, like he's wondering if I know what I'm getting myself into. I wish I had an answer.

When I keep my fucking mouth shut, he raises his glass again. "To Herself, then."

I drink to Alix. And I wonder if Leo will get out of this alive.

3

ALIX

I'm sitting at my desk in the freeport office building, playing back video from the professional-quality camera that arrived this morning. I told Trap I didn't need such a fancy machine; my phone would do just fine for whatever I have to record. But he insisted on buying the best—an investment we'll use over and over as we promote freeport auctions to our clients.

I think he wanted it to distract me. To keep me from dwelling on lawyers and police, on the investigation into Klaus Herzog's murder. Like any physical object could make me forget the paparazzi who crowd the freeport gate, the sickening free-loaders who want to turn my personal hell into another internet news cycle.

The video camera *did* take me hours to figure out, but I've finally filmed three uninterrupted minutes of the wall across from my desk. I've also mastered attaching the camera to its tripod, zooming in on details, and fading to black at the end of a shot.

"I'm ready for my close-up."

I look up to find Trap framed in the doorway. His white dress shirt glows in golden light from the sunset behind me. Hints of brown and gold gleam in his near-black hair. The light brings out the jade in his jungle eyes.

I turn off the camera. "I didn't realize how late it is."

"You know you're a salaried employee, right? The freeport doesn't pay overtime."

I appreciate that he's trying to keep things light, but I have to ask, "How did your meeting go?"

He closes the office door. I might not be the only freeport employee working late, and some things shouldn't be overheard.

"Kelly's in."

An iron rod melts in the column of my spine. I didn't realize how anxious I was, how much I feared the handsome Irish mobster would refuse to get involved.

I want Leo. I need Leo. But I don't want Trap going anywhere near the Herzog brothers on his own.

"When?" I ask.

"Next Saturday."

"But that's—"

"Only eight days," he interrupts.

Leo's been at the Philadelphia address for three years. There's no reason for anyone to move him in the next week. But now that I know my brother's alive, I don't want to wait for my revenge.

"Come over here," Trap says.

My body is conditioned to obey his command. I cross the room without making a conscious decision to do so. Just two nights ago, Trap and I made love without any power play at all, setting aside our usual dynamics of dominance and submission, the ones that make my blood sing. The bond between us that night was deeper than anything I've ever experienced in my life. More solid. More pure.

That's the connection that ignites every nerve in my body as Trap cups the back of my head. He tilts my neck until I'm staring right into his shadowed green eyes. "I know how much this means to you. I understand. But we need to make sure we can do the job safely. On Long Island…"

On Long Island, Sawgrass Corporation sent a team of its best men, an assassination squad determined to take out the Herzogs before they could do more harm. Eight Sawgrass men died, and three more are still in the hospital.

Eight deaths, eleven families changed forever, all because of me.

What the hell am I doing? How can I put more men at risk to retrieve Leo? What will I do if Trap doesn't come back from Philadelphia?

"Alix," Trap says, his voice a stern warning. How does he do that? How does he read my mind? His fingers still press into my hair, but now it feels like he's holding me back instead of reassuring me.

"I'll go there alone," I say. "I'll get him out."

"The fuck you will," Trap says.

I have to convince him. Protect him. "No one will expect me to show up there. It'll be a lot easier that way. A lot safer."

"Safer for who?" Trap asks, and nothing about his question is safe. His wrist has tightened, like he's trying to keep from crushing my skull.

I know he won't hurt me. Trap will never hurt me, not without my consent—and he'll only do that in the twisted sexual world we both need.

But I wouldn't put it past him to lock me away. To keep me someplace safe and secure, where he knows the Herzogs can never reach me.

"Safer for who, Alix?" He repeats his question, standing close enough to bite me. Heat radiates off his body like he's a nuclear blast furnace.

I fight to keep from turning away, from sheltering my face from the storm. "For you," I whisper.

His jaw tightens and his hand shakes. "*You* don't keep *me* safe. That's not your job."

"But—"

"That's never your job," he says.

And then his lips are hard against mine, punishing. I have to open to him, have to give him my tongue, my teeth, my breath. He walks me back until my desk digs into the backs of my thighs. He presses more, so I'm sitting, and he plants his arms around me.

He's a volcano seething toward eruption. A tornado. A hurricane. I moan beneath him, my determination to retrieve my brother scoured away by Trap's greater will.

That sound ignites something inside him, and he sweeps a stack of papers off my desk. I gasp in alarm, barely catching the new camera before it goes flying too. I clutch it to my chest, heart pounding.

"What the fuck is that?" Trap asks, and I think he might throw it across the room just to get his hands on my breasts.

"The video camera," I say. "The new one."

His eyes gleam. "Show me."

The order rockets into all the melted places inside me. I have no doubt what he's asking. He doesn't want a lesson on how the camera works. He wants to make a video of me. Of us. He wants to film us having sex.

The past three months have taught me Trap's commands always lead to freedom, to a wild release of the tension that's even now spinning from my belly to my thighs, literally curling my toes in anticipation.

But we're talking about a *camera*.

When I was a slave, Klaus Herzog filmed me without my knowledge or permission. He caught the most degrading moments of my life on video. I was an animal to him. A dumb beast with no free will.

"Show. Me." Trap repeats his order with the absolute certainty he's used for every command he's ever given me in bed.

And that's why this is different. Herzog didn't ask for my participation. He didn't let me make a decision. But with Trap I know I always have a choice. If I use my safeword, if I say *red*, Trap will put the camera down and walk out of my office without hesitation. He won't punish me, physically or emotionally.

So I show him.

I show him how the camera attaches to its tripod. I show him how to focus on the foreground, on the background, on the middle space between. I show him how to touch the red-lined button, how to hit *record*.

And when the camera's running, when its unblinking eye is watching everything we do, I let Trap issue more commands.

I work the buttons on my top, the top three at least, until he loses patience and rips open the last four.

I let him bind my wrists with my torn shirt, and I flex my fingers as he yanks his knots tighter.

I present my breasts—my "fucking incredible tits"—squeezing them between my biceps like ripe melons on a tray.

I'm wearing a sports bra—he didn't count on that. There aren't any hooks to rip open to give him the instant access he always fights for. He grunts and shoves the bra up to my chin, letting the fabric bunch around my throat. I immediately look at the camera, knowing I must look ridiculous.

"Eyes on me," Trap says.

I obey. And that means I catch the satisfied flare in Trap's feral gaze. "Good girl, Princess," he says, and his approval shouldn't light a fire deep inside me. I shouldn't desire that type of approval. I'm not a girl. I'm not a princess. I'm a free-thinking, strong and independent woman. But I know I'll do just about anything to hear Trap's praise again.

I know he bound my hands for a reason, but he left them in

front of me, instead of forcing them behind my back. I take advantage of his oversight.

I arch my back to emphasize the breasts that Trap finds so distracting. He mutters a few filthy words, stoking the flame he's already kindled in the soaked V between my thighs. I tighten my arms again, and he accepts the engraved invitation—I yelp as his teeth close around my right nipple. He sucks hard, cheeks hollowing as electric paths light up throughout my body.

With his attention fully focused on the hard pebble he's teasing, I use my bound fingers to work the button on my jeans. I moan his name, loud enough to cover the sizzle of my zipper easing down. I slip my fingers inside my plain cotton panties and find my throbbing clit.

He catches my hand before I manage a single stroke of relief. "What the fuck do you think you're doing?"

"Please…" I beg, not caring how desperate I sound.

"Did I say you could touch yourself?"

"I thought—"

"Did you ask my permission?"

"No, I—"

"What should we do with a girl who breaks the rules?"

He can walk away—he's done that before. He can jerk himself to orgasm and leave me desperate—he knows I can't come without his command. He can do whatever he wants with me, that's what I've offered, that's what I've given, and that's what the camera is capturing forever.

I flex my fingers, reaching for his belt buckle. "Let me make you feel good," I say, longing for the moment when he tells me he wants my mouth or my palms or the hot, wet channel that aches inside me.

But he takes a step back. He denies me the contact I need.

"Forearms on the seat," he says, pointing toward the simple armchair I keep for coworkers who visit my office.

"Please—" I try again.

"Forearms," is his only response.

I do what he says. The motion, of course, leaves my butt in the air. He yanks down my unbuttoned pants. His grip closes on my panties. He tugs hard, but the fabric is too sturdy to rip. I yelp at the contact with my over-sensitive clit which—predictably—makes him tug again.

I hold my breath and tighten my belly. I close my eyes to concentrate more on the pressure I need. I shift my feet, widening my stance and finding a better angle for his next pull.

Only then do I realize he's stepped away. I hear him riffling through things on my desk—my phone, my stapler—and I start to stand up straight.

"If your arms leave that chair one more time, I'm tying you to the fucking desk and going home for the night."

I glue my arms to the chair.

He must find what he's looking for because he returns to my side. I barely have time to brace myself before a searing flame kisses my left hip.

No. Not flame.

Ice.

My ears are filled with the rasp of sawing, and I realize Trap is cutting through my panties, levering a pair of steel scissors against my over-heated flesh. One slice on the left, another on the right, and he pulls my mangled underwear free.

My ass is bare for the camera. I wonder how he's set the focus, if he's zoomed in the lens to capture every detail. Is he filming my aching lower lips? Is he focused on the tight stone of my clit? Is the camera showing the honeyed sheen I smell as I drop my head onto my bound wrists?

"Count," Trap says, giving me only a second to brace for what I should have expected all along.

The flat of his belt falls high on my ass like the opening note of a symphony. "One," I call, loud and clear because I want the camera to catch the sound.

Another blow, a full octave below, laying a stripe across the top of my thighs. "Two," I announce, proud and strong.

A third, perfecting a balanced chord. "Three," I manage after I catch my breath.

Four.

My ass burns.

Five.

My knees shake.

Six.

My toes dig in to keep me balanced.

Seven.

Trap's crescendo builds.

Eight.

I'm whining. Begging. Adding a chorus without words to the symphony soaring through my flesh.

Nine.

Every note melts into a perfect harmonic convergence, echoing, complementing, expanding into something greater than each individual strand. I'm held by the music, sustained by the waves. I'm deep inside my body and soaring far overhead. I'm waiting and waiting and waiting—

Ten.

I try to remember how to move my tongue, how to shape my lips, how to form the word that Trap requires.

But he speaks before I can: "Come."

And I rise. I fall. I shatter into a million separate notes.

My knees buckle. My striped ass rocks back, settles on my heels, burning, throbbing, as wave after wave rolls through my core.

I chant Trap's name like a prayer. I try to remember how to breathe.

And still, my arms stay pinned to the seat of the chair. My fingers grasp the fabric. My knuckles turn to stone.

He kneels beside me. He reaches for the fabric that binds my wrists. He releases the knots and eases off the cloth. And he sits back against my desk, pulling me into his lap, folding his arms around me and rocking me until the shudders finally slow.

I follow the rules.

I'm Trap's good girl.

And the camera catches it all, every single second, because he loves me and I love him, and this is the world we've built together.

4

TRAP

Sweet fucking Jesus.

Sitting on the side of my bed, I tap the screen on my phone, zeroing out the video. I've watched it a dozen times over the last week, and every viewing shows me something I missed before.

The desperate tilt of Alix's hips as she assumes the position I command, instinctively sheltering her sensitive clit.

The way her fingers clench as she anticipates the second slash of my belt.

The tiny moan she swallows before she says nine.

My cock apparently thinks I'm a sixteen-year-old kid. I'm hard again, even though I beat off in the shower just thirty minutes ago. And Alix took care of my morning wood as the sun rose over the treeline in the backyard, before either of us was fully awake. And she blew me last night, after I finally unbuckled the gag I made her wear for an extra-long session with a vibrator.

I guess that means Alix is acting like a horny kid too.

So my plan fucking worked.

Plan. That makes it sound like I thought the whole thing out ahead of time. Like I knew the camera had arrived while I was up in Philly, setting up my extracurricular activity with Kelly.

It was a surprise to me. But the second I saw it in her hands, I knew what I had to do. What I *wanted* to do. What I prayed would work for her.

My poor princess… She still refuses to let me see anything that Herzog filmed. She says it won't change anything. It won't wash away what happened in that fucking hellhole. It'll just make me blind with rage.

She's probably right about that. The thought of any man touching her… Of Herzog forcing her for three fucking years…

But I know she watches those goddamn tapes. She copied them over to her laptop. She said she was making sure evidence wouldn't be lost if anything happens to Herzog's computer.

She thinks I don't notice her going into the guest room. She makes excuses about getting something out of the closet, about trying on shoes, about some other lie I pretend to believe. But her face is pale as milk when she comes out. And she rubs her fucking wrist like she's still wearing the electronic cuff that cocksucker used to summon her.

I can't erase the three years she spent in hell.

I can't destroy the videos, not without making her even more ashamed.

But when I saw the new camera last Friday, a fucking devil planted his pitchfork in my brain. We can make our own videos, Alix and me. I can show her how gorgeous she is. How strong she is. How she can do more, take more, *be* more than she ever imagined.

My finger hovers over my phone. One more viewing before I head up to Philly…

I'm about to give in to sweet temptation when Alix comes into the room. Her whiskey eyes look bright, like someone lit a candle deep inside a cave. Her cheeks are flushed too. I'm pretty sure that if I put the back of my hand on her forehead, she'd feel like a feverish child. "Shouldn't you be gone by now?" she asks.

I mime a shot to my heart. "Ow."

She doesn't smile. "You said you're meeting Braiden at ten."

I glance at the clock on the nightstand. "It isn't even eight yet."

"You can't be late."

"It's a ninety-minute drive. Less if I break the speed limit."

"You can't break the speed limit!" She looks like I told her I'm taking out full-page ads in the *Philadelphia Enquirer*, the *New York Times*, and the *Washington Post*, advertising my plan for the night.

I cross the room, taking the chance to shove my phone and its video deep in my pocket. I smooth her hair off her face and cup the back of her head with both hands. I wait until her jittery eyes focus on me and then I squeeze with just enough pressure to let her know I'm here for her. I'm never going to let her go.

"I won't break the speed limit," I say. "I'm not even sure the van can go that fast."

"Which van?" She looks like she's taking inventory of the entire freeport garage.

"The one I bought two days ago," I say patiently. "Paying cash to a used car lot in fucking Baltimore. The one I had trucked into the freeport after hours last night. The one I pegged with plates stolen from a nursing home in Ocean City."

She's not listening. She's already neck-deep in her next imagined nightmare. "How can we trust Braiden's men? We don't know them. What would it take for them to double-cross you? They could be texting Jonas and Ansel right now—"

I shift a hand to settle a finger over her lips. "Braiden Kelly has been Philadelphia's captain for the last five years. He trusts his men with his life—over a hell of a lot more than a single raid on a single warehouse on a single dock near the Navy Yard."

"But—"

"Those men are his brothers."

"They aren't *your* brothers."

"Kelly's in the Diamond Ring. He was there the night Herzog died. His ass is on the line with the video too. That's good enough for me." I hesitate just a moment, but I figure she needs to know the rest. "Don't be fooled by Kelly's lilting accent and his baby blues. He's the real deal—Irish mob. One of his men goes rogue, and Kelly'll be first in line to cut off the motherfucker's dick. Feed it to him through a fucking straw, then take out the guy's wife. Kids, too. All the rest of his family. It's a fucking code, and every one of those bastards knows the rules."

Alix doesn't flinch. She's already spinning out her next made-up disaster. "There might be more men in the warehouse than you expect. What if there's a big delivery tonight? Jonas and Ansel might show up for an inspection. Maybe—"

I pull her close, smothering her speculation against my black sweater. Her shoulders stiffen, and she braces to push away, but I only tighten my arms. Her hands are caught between us; I feel her claws against my chest. I touch my lips to her hair and hold her fast.

"It'll all be fine," I murmur. "I'll be back before dawn."

"Don't go," she whispers.

"I have to."

"Tell Braiden I need you here."

"You don't."

She clutches my sweater like she's about to rip it off my body. She leans back enough to meet my gaze. "Be careful," she says, her voice catching in a broken hiccup.

I bend down to kiss her, just a brush of my lips against hers. Anything more, and she'll think I'm saying goodbye forever. Closing my hands around her elbows, I take a full step away. "We'll laugh about this in the morning."

She doesn't say anything.

There's nothing I can say to convince her. I just have to go.

She follows me into my closet. She watches as I push aside the row of tailored suits. I had the gun safe installed three years ago, after she went missing—like the comfort of a Sig Sauer could make up for the open wound deep inside my heart.

That explains the four-digit combination she watches me punch in: 0621. Her birthday. The night we met.

The safe gives its familiar electronic chime, and the door clicks open. The gun is exactly the way I left it, fully loaded, sitting on a padded rest, waiting to stop a thief or a charging vampire.

I strap on the waiting shoulder holster. Pick up the gun. Add an extra clip to the holster.

The safe chimes again when I close it. I shove the suits into place and turn to Alix. "Don't wait up," I say. It's a piss-poor joke, because we both know there's no way in fucking hell she's going to sleep before I get home.

This time when I kiss her, neither one of us holds back. She meets my tongue, fierce and proud. My palm cups the back of her neck, like I can melt our bodies together. I want to drown in her forever.

We pull away at the same time. My fingers trace the line of her jaw. She catches my hand and squeezes once, hard enough to pinch bone.

And then she steps away and I head out to capture her miserable son-of-a-bitch of a brother.

5

ALIX

I wait in the house until midnight. I hover in my office over in the freeport tower until three, staring at my computer screen, studying the security feed from the front gate. I spend two and a half hours pacing the warehouse loading dock.

Every few minutes, I take out my phone and check the display in case I missed the reassuring buzz of an incoming message from Trap. Nothing. Not a word. Which might mean everything has gone perfectly and he has nothing to report.

And it might mean disaster.

The white panel van finally arrives at 5:27. At least at this hour on a Sunday morning, the paparazzi are still sleeping. There's no crowd outside the freeport gates, no eager photographers waiting for a money shot of me, the Steak Knife Killer.

I'm at the driver-side door before the vehicle comes to a stop. My stomach seizes as I look in the window. Trap leans forward in his seat, forehead resting against the steering wheel.

"Oh my God!" I grab for the door handle, but it's locked.

He looks up. It takes him a moment, but he opens the door.

His face is pale. His eyes are rimmed with red, like he's pulled an all-nighter before the most important college exam of his academic career. He moves like a prizefighter at the end of a twelve-round match.

But his feet touch the ground. He hauls himself out of the van. He stands upright. And he stays standing as I throw myself at his chest.

I don't know what I'm saying, what I'm asking; all my words run together. But Trap's hand is soothing as he cups the back of my head. He murmurs something: "It's okay. I'm home now. It's okay."

I let myself melt into his reassurance. I inhale his unique scent of rosemary and ice. I allow myself to believe that everything will be all right.

And then I realize he's wearing a gray sweatshirt. It's too tight across his chest. The sleeves are too short. He left the freeport dressed all in black.

Stepping back, I steady myself by grabbing his biceps. He winces, almost too quickly for me to notice. "What happened?" I ask, looking at his hands, his arms, his legs. "Where are you hurt?"

"I'm fine," he says.

"What happened?" I ask again, and I hear the shaking in my voice, but there's no way to stop it. When he doesn't answer quickly enough, I say, "Trap—"

"I'm fine," he repeats. "There were only two men. Two men and Leo."

"Are they…" I don't want to say the word *dead.* Dead sounds rude. Dead is final. I grew up in a world where I could never imagine needing to ask the question.

"The two guys, yeah."

"Did you…"

He shakes his head. "Kelly got one. His lieutenant got the

other. But one of the shitstains got off a few shots before he was taken out."

"Trap!"

He squares his shoulders, clearly making an effort to look okay. "It's a graze," he says, like he twisted an ankle, or maybe got a sunburn. "Nothing serious. It just bled like a motherfucker."

"You need a doctor!"

"Kelly keeps a guy on call. I'm all stitched up. Good as new. He gave me a tetanus shot and everything."

He's trying to keep me calm. And because it's Trap, because I know his voice, because I'm used to listening and doing what he says, it works. But I have to ask, "Kelly? And his man?"

"They're fine. I got the worst of it."

"A— and Leo?"

Trap's jaw tightens. He juts his chin toward the back of the van. "He's back there. And you need to know—he's high as a kite."

Of course he is. My blood steams in my veins.

Leo is the reason Trap got shot tonight. Braiden and his men could have died up there in Philly. I could have lost Trap forever. All because my brother is in the Herzogs' pockets.

I'm not even thinking. My hands are on the back of the van, ready to turn the handle, to yank open the door and get my fingers around Leo's neck. But Trap stops me with a single low word: "Princess!"

I stare at him, blinking.

He nods toward the warehouse proper. "You've got a room ready?"

"Yes, but—"

"Get the door open. The sun'll be up in half an hour. We don't need any random clients seeing him. Knowing what's going on."

He's right, of course. Freeport business is conducted 24/7/365. Leo must be hidden from freeport clients and staff alike. But my palms itch as I use my employee ID to open the door from the loading dock.

Trap planned big when he built the warehouse. There are six stories underground, each equipped with a dozen state-of-the-art, climate-controlled, electronics-shielded galleries. Freeport clients can store anything on the premises—we're a strictly don't-ask-don't-tell enterprise. Each gallery is a safe deposit box the size of a shipping container, protected by retina scans, fingerprint biometrics, and voice activation.

I told Trap I didn't want him involved in the gallery I created for Leo. I didn't want Trap to see the gynecological exam table I ordered, paying nearly three times the cost for overnight delivery. I didn't want to watch him speculate about the stainless-steel stirrups. I didn't want him to think about hard metal cuffs sawing into wrists and ankles, about blinding lights left on around the clock, about a cheap plastic bucket waiting to be filled with piss and shit.

I know all of that.

I *lived* all of that.

But I wanted to spare Trap as long as I possibly could.

I press my forehead against the electronic reader, opening my eyes wide for the laser scan. I roll my fingertips across the sensitive pad. I swallow hard and speak my name, trying to enunciate over the pounding of my heart: "Alix Key."

A lock opens deep inside the door. I set my palm against the inches-thick steel. It's so perfectly weighted that I barely need to flex my wrist to make it swing open.

The gallery is an exact replica of Klaus Herzog's Holding Room where I was chained for ninety days. Ninety days of rape. Ninety days of torture. Ninety days as a prologue to three long years.

All because Leo couldn't stay clean. Because my brother needed drugs. Because my twin sold me to make good on his own debt.

My gallery is pristine. Freeport maintenance staff bolted my table to the floor, asking no questions because Trap requires absolute loyalty. I tested the soundproofing myself, screaming as loud as I could while an Oscar-award-winning sound engineer waited outside with a decibel meter. I panted for nearly an hour behind the closed, locked door, doing my best to approximate hyperventilation while testing the air handling system.

Everything's ready.

Everything's waiting.

I know time is of the essence. We need to get Leo down here. We need to get the van out of the loading dock. We need to finish our transaction before anyone stumbles on what we've done.

But I linger in the doorway, my hand on the light switch. It's not too late. I can still change my mind. Trap and I haven't done anything—yet—that we can't take back.

Tomorrow, I won't be able to say the same. Or the next day. Or the one after that.

Leo's going to detox here. Alone. Unaided. No doctors or group therapy or pharmaceutical support.

Maybe it will kill him.

I hope it doesn't. I hope he makes it to ninety days. I hope he survives longer than he ever lasted at rehab, any one of the eight times I scrimped and saved and tried to rescue him.

Because on the ninetieth day, I'm going to kill him.

Me. Just me.

After all, I'm the one who killed Klaus Herzog. I murdered him in a frenzy—all fire and blood. I discovered an opportunity, and I took it before I could be enslaved for the rest of my life.

Leo won't die the same way. No knife across the throat. No blood arcing to the ceiling. No mad scramble as his insides are shredded.

I'm going to kill Leo like the animal he is. I'm going to stop his heart with a single injection, straight into a vein. It's more mercy than he deserves.

I leave the gallery door ajar and head back to the loading

dock. Trap is sitting in the driver's seat, his knees outside the door. He sighs as he hauls himself upright.

He must be exhausted. *I'm* running on adrenaline, and I haven't driven back and forth to Philadelphia, been caught in a shoot-out, or suffered a wound bad enough to need stitches. Once we get Leo locked away, I'll take Trap back to the house. I'll get him out of that too-small sweatshirt and load him up with painkillers or a double-shot of whiskey, whichever he prefers.

"Ready?" he asks.

I nod, even though I'm afraid I'm not strong enough. But if Trap takes Leo's arms, carries the weight of his head and his chest… I should be able to hold onto his feet. I hope. I pray.

Trap opens the back door of the van.

Leo is in a wheelchair. Four steel clips on the inside of the van anchor heavy ropes, securing the chair against rolling during transport. A thick strap is fastened around my brother's chest, holding him upright. His arms and legs are bound to the chair's metal frame. A shapeless black hood covers his head. His neck is bent at a sharp angle, like his nose is made out of a three-ton weight.

I can't see his face. His wrists are thin, like they belong to a scarecrow. He's wearing a T-shirt that used to be white, and his jogging pants are filthy. A heavy wet stain announces that he peed himself, and the stench tells me he lost control of his bowels too.

I make a strangled sound, a question that I don't know how to put into words. Trap doesn't answer. Instead, he hauls himself into the van. He pushes a metal ramp out of the cargo compartment, clanging it to the ground and setting a dangerously steep angle for the wheelchair.

"Let's go, shitbird," he says to Leo. He works the heavy metal clips, kicking the ropes away from the chair's wheels.

"Careful," Trap says to me. I see his lips start to purse, start to form the word *Princess* but he stops before he breathes another syllable.

Leo, though, realizes someone else is on the dock. "Who's there?" he calls.

His voice is as familiar as my own. It's filled with fear, of course. And he slurs his words. He's high. Trap said that. But I have no doubt that's my brother under that hood. That's my twin.

Trap pushes the chair down the ramp, not bothering to cushion the jolt at the bottom. Leo grunts, or maybe that's a whine. He twists his head to the left and then to the right. "Is someone out there? Help me. Please, help me. This man is trying to kill me. Please!"

Please. That's the last word I heard Leo say in Herzog's mansion—right before I was raped the first time.

"Okay?" Trap asks. I wonder what my face looks like, to make him sound so worried.

I nod.

Trap starts to wheel the chair into the warehouse.

"Someone?" Leo asks. "Anyone?" And then he shouts, "Hey! Can you hear me? Is anyone there! Help!"

Trap slaps the hood with an open palm. "Shut the fuck up, asshole."

Leo quiets down.

I can't allow myself to feel sorry for him. Forget about what Leo did to *me*. He's a rapist. He preyed on slaves in Herzog's mansion, conned innocent women with candy bars. Those women were my sisters. Siblings by choice, after what my blood brother did to me.

Trap pushes the chair through the door. Down the hall. Into the elevator, which takes us three stories underground.

The gallery door is still ajar, just the way I left it. Trap turns the chair around and takes the door with his shoulders, backing into the room. He nods for me to close the steel barrier behind him, and all three of us hear the locking mechanism engage.

"Where am I?" Leo asks. "What are you doing to me?"

He's crying now. His words are thick and gristly, like the garbage left on the edge of a bloody plate. "Please…" he begs again.

How many women begged him for mercy?

Trap wheels him around to face the center of the room.

"Holy shit," Trap says. I watch him take in the table, the stirrups, the heavy steel bands at the top and bottom of the flat metal surface. He glances toward a rolling cart, tools I'll only need tonight. Things I can't trust Leo with, once Trap and I leave. "Sweet fucking Jesus…"

"What?" Leo asks, his voice cracking in terror. "What are you doing to me? Help!" He screams again, the sound bouncing off the flat white ceiling.

Trap closes his hand around Leo's throat. "Shut the fuck up," he growls.

Leo doesn't try to scream again. But his sobs grow louder—heavy, wracking gasps that make his whole body shudder. The stench from his pants burns the roof of my mouth, and I glance at the bucket in the corner. He's going to live with that reek for three full months.

That's nothing, compared to what happens to the children taking the drugs he sold. Herzog developed Crash specifically to target adolescents, boys and girls whose brains weren't yet fully formed. Every dose Leo sold preyed on innocents. He's a monster.

A monster who doesn't resist as Trap wheels him over to the table. "Try anything," Trap says, "and I'll break your fucking fingers. Understand?"

When Leo doesn't answer, Trap slaps the back of his head. "Got it, dickhead?"

"I've got it," Leo weeps.

He ruined my life. Ruined my family. Ruined how many other families—siblings and parents and other loved ones desperate to hear from Herzog's slaves, from his broken, addicted customers.

Trap unties Leo's legs first. Then his arms. Then, finally, the heavy strap around his chest.

Leo doesn't move until Trap starts to wrestle him onto the table. Then, my brother thrashes, scrambling like a damaged crab. Trap gets him in a headlock, clamping hard around his neck. "Go on, cumwipe. Just try it. I'll break your fucking neck."

Leo's arms and legs sag like newly poured concrete. He still moves; his chest is heaving, his belly rising and falling like he's just run a hundred-meter sprint.

I know that type of gasping. That's the way I felt every time Herzog cornered me. Every time he penetrated me—with his cock, with his fist, with any cruel item he happened to have around. That's the way I felt every time he made me bleed. Made me scream.

Leo doesn't resist as Trap fastens the bonds around his wrists. He doesn't fight as his feet go into the stirrups. He barely moans as the metal bonds saw into the filthy flesh of his ankles.

His feet are bare. Did he have shoes when they found him in Philadelphia? Did Trap take them away, to keep him from running?

No. The soles of Leo's feet are black. He hasn't worn shoes in a very long time.

Once my brother is secure, Trap looks toward the rolling rack. He raises his eyebrows and tilts his head. He's asking if I want to do the honors.

I pick up a pair of heavy-duty shears. I'm going to cut off Leo's clothes, leave him cold and naked and alone. But my hands are shaking so hard I can't slip my fingers through the grips.

Trap waits, giving me a chance to recover.

I want this. I need this. I deserve revenge.

But I can't move. I can't make my hands manage the scissors.

Trap takes them from me. Leo's grimy T-shirt fabric melts beneath the blades like ice in a furnace. The waistband of his sweatpants offers token resistance, but the shears make short work of both disgusting legs. Leo isn't wearing underpants.

He's lying in his own shit. His feet are pinned in the stirrups. His tiny penis tries to crawl inside the bellows of his belly as his knees knock together in cruel imitation of protection.

"Why are you doing this?" he whimpers. "What did I do? Please, just tell me what I did! Please!"

I can't decide where to begin. *You stole my family. You stole my friends. You stole my fiancé and then, when I found a man a million times better, you stole three years I could have spent with him. You gave me nightmares I'm still unable to put into words. My body tore because of you. My blood spilled. You turned me into a murderer, because that was the only way I could ever be free.*

Trap has moved to the top of the table. His hand is poised over Leo's head. His fingers stretch toward the heavy black fabric.

He waits for me to meet his storm-dark green-brown gaze. And when I nod, he rips away the hood.

6

TRAP

~

Leo Fucking Key is a goddamn mess. His hair hangs down to his shoulders, individual strands melted into thick, filthy hanks. His beard grew in patchy, but it's matted together too. He's got an open sore on his right cheekbone; something that looks like it started as a burn before it went red and oozing. He broke his nose at some point, and no one bothered to set it.

His eyes are so dilated all I can see is black, not a hint of the whiskey brown I know so well from Alix. He's shaking like he's in one of those rock tumblers I begged my parents for when I was a kid. The goose pimples on his arms are bigger than his pitiful prick.

Herzog's guys kept him chained to a table; his neck is scarred from an iron collar. When Kelly's lieutenant kicked in the door, one of the jailers yanked Leo to his feet by his hair. The cumstain used him as a shield, which might have worked if Kelly hadn't gotten off a perfect head-shot.

Now, the broomstick of Leo's neck is twisted around so he's

gaping at me. His jaw is slack and his mouth smells like ass; I don't know how many teeth he has left, but at least one of them is rotting.

He blinks hard, trying to focus in the glare of the room. I crush the hood in my fist as it takes him three tries to ask, "Who *are* you?"

Because he's staring at me, he doesn't see Alix take two steps forward. He doesn't know her hand stretches out. He can't tell that her fingers grasp empty air. But a tiny noise rips out of her throat, something between a gasp and a sob and that's when he finally turns toward her.

"Alix?" He sounds like a little boy, finally catching his first glance of Santa Claus or the Easter Bunny or the Tooth Fairy.

She doesn't say a word.

"Alix?" he asks again, his ruined face lighting up from inside. "Master said he killed you. He said you were dead."

She flinches at *Master*, a full-body twist. "He's not your fucking master," she says, every syllable etched in acid.

I've heard her swear plenty of times. Hell, I taught her most of the words she knows. But there's something about this *fucking* —it's raw and dangerous, and I suddenly remember that the scissors weren't the only tools on that rolling table.

There's a steak knife there, lean and dangerous, and if it's not the one she used to execute Herzog, it's part of the same set. She has a scalpel too, something she must have ordered when she had the goddamn medical table delivered.

Stirrups. She's got him in fucking stirrups, his shit-smeared ass half off the table.

Leo gulps for air like a beached goldfish. "He said he killed you. He said he had to because I fucked up. I lied to him. I said you were a virgin."

Alix flicks a glance toward me. She left *my* bed that night. She went home wearing *my* boxers, *my* T-shirt. She must have arrived home smelling like sex. That's what doomed her.

No.

Leo doomed her.

"It was none of your fucking business," Alix says. Again, her voice is frozen. Each word sounds like it could shatter into a million diamond-sharp points.

"I'm sorry," Leo sobs. "I'm so, so sorry. I told him I was wrong. I told him it was my fault. I begged for him to let you go. I tried!"

"Not hard enough. Did it ever cross your mind to call the fucking cops?"

"I didn't have a chance! He kept me in the house until he killed you and then—"

"I'm not dead!" She shouts it loud enough for my ears to ring.

Leo shakes his head like he doesn't believe her. Maybe it's the fucking Crash in his system. He was already begging me for a fix while Kelly was putting insurance shots in the brains of both the guys babysitting him.

Him, and a hundred keys of Crash.

"I'm not dead," Alix says again and this time her voice is back to ice. The man chained to the table between us might as well be a stranger. A mannequin. An actor in a film.

She's not dead. But Leo might be before she and I walk out of this room.

"I know that now," Leo says. "But I thought you were. He showed me pictures. A woman. Her head was cut off, and her puss—, her v— vagina was in shreds. He said he used a firecracker, a Sky King. He showed me the box, honest!"

Alix doesn't react, not visibly. But I have to swallow twice to get the acid out of my throat. I hope to hell Herzog had a special effects guy on his payroll, someone who could make a fake corpse to fool Leo.

I know he didn't.

"After you d—," Leo says, and then he corrects himself before Alix can set the record straight once again. "After I *thought* you were dead, he sent me to the warehouse. He said I could work off my debt. A month for stealing and I'd be free. But he gave me another month when I fucked up a package of meth. And a month after that when I got the runs and couldn't work. After that...after that, he didn't make excuses anymore. He just kept me there. Just made me work."

Alix knows her sentence was originally three days. She knows it stretched to three years and would have gone longer if she hadn't saved herself.

But that's the thing.

She *did* save herself. She figured out a way to be free.

So when she looks at the pitiful creature chained to her table, when she sees her brother's snot running into his mouth, when she sees his bony knees shaking above those stirrups like he's got a fucking vibrator jammed up his ass, she has to wonder why she was strong enough to escape and Leo wasn't. Why she killed Herzog and Leo packaged the motherfucker's drugs. Why she's walking the freeport like a royal fucking princess, and he's pleading for his goddamn life.

Alix looks at me for the first time since I pulled the hood off her brother. "Let's go," she says. And she turns toward the exit.

Leo must be so surprised he forgets to plead until Alix's hand is on the doorknob. "Don't leave me here!" he begs.

Alix's fingers tense.

"Please!" he cries.

She turns the knob beneath her palm. Opens the door. Juts her chin to tell me to go first.

"At least give me my fix!" Leo shouts. "Just a little something. Take the edge off. Please!"

The sound of his begging cuts off as the door snicks closed between us.

Alix stands in the hallway, her face drained. I thought I knew every one of her emotions. I thought I could read her like a shipping contract. But I don't have a clue what she's thinking now.

I'm thinking I need to clear the loading dock. Kelly and I agreed I'd take care of the white van. Drive it down to East Baltimore. Wipe it down for prints, take the stolen license plates, and leave the keys in the ignition. Torch the fucking plates after Amtrak gets me home.

The silence gets thicker. Heavier. The stitches in my left shoulder are starting to ache. Too bad I didn't follow doctor's orders and drink plenty of fluids, get a full night's sleep.

She's still standing there. Debating. Fighting a demon I'll never truly understand.

I need to get to a computer. Check the news. Read my email. Jonas and Ansel Herzog won't accept what happened tonight without a battle. Kelly and I, we went into enemy territory. We stole enemy goods—Leo and the two hundred pounds of Crash that Kelly's presumably stowing away right now. We killed enemy soldiers.

The question isn't *whether* there'll be hell to pay. The question is *when*. And just how fucking bad it'll be.

"Alix," I finally say.

"I hate him."

"I know."

"I want him to suffer exactly the way I did. I want him to be that scared. That hurt. That alone."

"I know."

"I want him so broken he can't imagine there's a way out, so hopeless he doesn't dream anymore when he sleeps."

"Princess—"

"But he's still my brother. I don't want to, but I love him."

She's crying now, silent tears leaking out of her eyes, painting her cheeks silver in the overhead light.

"I love the little boy he was. I love the best friend I had for years. I love the other half of me, the one I thought was gone forever because of all of Herzog's lies." Her hand is moving, squeezing an invisible something, like she's juicing a lemon or holding a beating heart.

My princess isn't an evil woman. She isn't cruel. She's

broken, damaged, and her soul may never heal from all the things she's survived. But she doesn't lie awake at night figuring out new ways to torture kittens and pluck the wings off butterflies.

She thought she could drown her past by locking Leo in that room. Now she knows it will never be that simple.

"Tell me," I say. "Whatever you want me to do, I'll do it."

I'll kill him for her.

I'll drive him back to Navy Yard, give him back to the Herzogs.

I'll leave him locked up, let Alix measure out every second of her revenge.

She swallows and raises her beautiful chin. "Call a doctor," she says. "Someone who can get here before he starts to seize."

7

ALIX

If life was a movie, everything would be wonderful right now. Leo would miraculously heal from his lifelong addictions. Trap would open the freeport doors to dozens of new clients, each one richer than the one before. I would channel the peace that naturally stems from forgiving my brother, discovering new insights into human emotions that I could channel into successful million-dollar auctions for freeport clients.

But life isn't a movie.

I wake in the middle of Sunday afternoon feeling hungover, even though Trap and I didn't touch a drop of alcohol after he got back from Philadelphia. A long shower doesn't help. Wearing my softest chenille socks doesn't help. Sipping chamomile tea with a generous dollop of manuka honey doesn't help.

Finally, I swap socks for sneakers and head over to the freeport warehouse.

The white van is gone from the loading dock. I take the

elevator down to the third floor. The security system on my gallery accepts my retina scan and fingerprints. The door clicks open when I say my name.

But the room inside is empty.

No examination table. No rolling cart. No plastic bucket in the corner. There's just a flat stretch of the freeport's featureless gray laminate floor. Maybe a hint of the rubbery smell of fresh paint.

I find Trap in the office tower, busy behind his desk. "Even God rested on the seventh day," I say.

He rubs his face as he looks up from his computer screen. He looks drained. "God didn't run a freeport."

I think of all the things I want to ask him. But instead I say, "What can I do to help?"

This is where he's supposed to make a joke. Snap his fingers and order me to my knees as he unzips his jeans. Tell me to sit on his face. But he just shrugs—apparently a bit too vigorously because he has to bite back a wince. "Everything's under control."

"I know that. When was the last time you ate?"

He thinks. "Dinner last night. No. I had to get the ramp for the van. Lunch."

"Yesterday?" I confirm, waiting for him to nod. "You're going to collapse."

"I'm not hungry."

Bullshit. That's what he would say. But I don't bother. Instead, I head down to the staff kitchen at the end of the hall. There are protein bars on the counter and a bowl filled with apples. I take one bar and two pieces of fruit, along with a bottle of plain water. I'm willing to bet he's drunk his body weight in energy drinks over the past twenty-four hours.

I put the food on his desk blotter, keeping an apple for myself. When I sink into the chair across from his desk, I take a huge bite, trying to slurp up the juice as noisily as possible.

Without looking up from his computer, Trap grabs his own apple. I try not to gloat as he finishes it in one minute flat.

I don't say a word until he's polished off the protein bar as well. The water disappears almost as quickly, all while he squints at his computer screen, completing some sort of online form. When he finally clicks on the big black box at the bottom, I ask, "What was that?"

"Health insurance enrollment."

"It couldn't wait till Susan's in tomorrow?" Susan Richards, his personal assistant, is a genius with online forms.

"It's for Leo."

He's protecting me—again. He's keeping the flawlessly discreet Susan from wondering why he's paying for my brother's insurance. He's avoiding any uncomfortable questions about treatment. About pre-existing conditions.

"Where is he?" I ask.

"Do you really want to know?"

I pause before answering. Knowing Leo's whereabouts is the first step toward letting him back in my life.

Second step, actually. Keeping him from dying in detox was the first.

"Yeah," I finally say. "I want to know."

"He's at Dover General. In a private suite."

"Hospitals have private suites?"

"They do if you pay enough."

I consider asking for more information. Who's his doctor? How are they treating him? Aside from the Crash, is he on other drugs?

But that all feels like too much. I know the whirlpool that perpetually spins around my brother. I can't let myself get sucked in to drown.

Instead, I say, "Thank you."

Trap just nods.

"How's your shoulder?"

"It feels like a rabid wolf tried to chew my arm off."

"You're sure it's not infected?"

"It's fine," he sighs. "Just hurts like a motherfucker. The doctor said it would. Shallow wounds are the worst."

Not worse than the ones that go straight through the heart. Or the brain. But he doesn't need me to argue.

A window flickers open on his computer screen—a text message. He palms it closed before I can see who sent it. I refuse to take the hint. "Who's that?"

He looks at me for nearly a minute, like he's trying to decide if I can live with the answer. Finally, he says, "Kelly."

"What's wrong?"

"Nothing."

"Why are you lying to me?"

"I'm not lying!" His voice is so sharp I cringe. He sees my flinch and he mutters something obscene. "I'm not lying," he repeats in a quieter voice. "The Herzogs found out he was involved in the raid. One of his own men must have talked. So now he gets to figure out if he's got a traitor on his hands or just a fucking moron. So much for laying low and visiting his Granny Muldoon in grand old County Limerick while the Herzogs cool down."

The Herzogs aren't going to cool down.

I reach across the desk and take Trap's right hand, the good one, so I don't have to worry about jostling his shoulder when I lace our fingers together. "Come back to the house," I ask.

He juts his chin toward the computer. "I've got work to do."

"You can work tomorrow. And the day after that. And so on and so on…"

He sighs from the very bottom of his lungs. I wonder if he got any sleep at all last night. I'm pretty sure not. "I have to—"

But whatever he's about to say is cut short by a yawn.

I squeeze his fingers. "Come to bed."

He shrugs again, and this time he can't cover up his wince. "I can't do you any good there."

"You can sleep, can't you? Beside me? We can turn on the

air conditioner and burrow under the blankets and pretend we're snowed into an Arctic cabin with nothing to do but sleep until the rescue team finds us."

"I need to…"

Maybe he's so tired he doesn't remember the end of the sentence. Maybe his to-do list is so long he can't choose which obligation comes next. Maybe he actually *has* reached the end of his tasks for the day.

But I take his trailing off as permission. I stand, still holding his hand. I tug, getting him to edge around his desk. We walk to the elevator, out the lobby door, and across the parking lot to the sleek brick wall of our home.

He follows me upstairs. He lets me take off his shirt and his jeans. He humors me when I gasp at the black thread of his stitches, and he pretends I don't sway a little on my feet as I imagine the doctor's needle pulling through his flesh.

We get into bed together. He curls around me, resting his heavy hand on my hip. I force myself to breathe evenly and deeply, doing everything in my power to lull him to sleep.

And when he's out, when his breath is heavy as a locomotive, when his fingers splay loosely across my leg, I stare at the clock as it flickers from minute to minute to minute.

I should feel good about helping Trap. I should be grateful that last night's raid in Philadelphia was as successful as it was. I should feel healed by my decision to save Leo, to let my brother live.

Instead, I feel drained.

Uncertain.

Empty.

And I can't think of a single way to solve that, even though I try to come up with something all afternoon and evening, well after the bedroom darkens with the autumn sunset.

8

TRAP

So, Alix was right.

I did need more to fuel my body than a fucking gallon of electric green Monster energy drink. And I didn't know how tired I was until I slept fourteen hours straight—through dinner, past midnight, only waking when the gray light before dawn leaks through the bedroom window.

I ease out of bed, grabbing a pair of sweatpants against the early morning chill. My shoulder is stiff as hell, and the stitches make it feel like I'm wearing a shirt three sizes too small. The doc said I'll have a bitch of a scar, which only seems fair if I feel this shitty. But I take a look in the mirror, and nothing's red or warm to the touch. So it looks like I'll live another day.

Downstairs, I raid the refrigerator. There's leftover chicken from dinner a few nights back; I can't remember exactly when, but it smells fine so I gulp it down with as little chewing as possible. I grab a fistful of grapes, then go back for half a bag of those baby carrots Alix loves. By then I'm in full vacuum mode, and pretty much nothing is safe. I finish by drinking milk straight from the carton.

All of which means I'm feeling pretty good when I sit down at my computer and log into my work account. And that's when the shit hits the fan.

Emails. Dozens of them—from every member of the Diamond Ring. But it's not just clients flooding my digital door. It's media too. It seems like every paper in the country—from the *New York Times* to the *Los Angeles Times*, along with TV, cable news shows, and God knows who else—wants me to comment.

My in-house lawyers are shitting bricks. My hired gun, the New York big dick who's representing me in the criminal investigation into Klaus Herzog's murder, has demanded that I call him immediately, on his private line.

Texts are rolling in too, at least one a minute as I try to shovel my way through the crap. It looks like primo Diamond Ring member Steve Torrington sent a message every five minutes from midnight on, ending with a five am instruction in all caps:

TAKE YOUR FUCKING DIAMOND RING AND
SHOVE IT SIDEWAYS UP YOUR ASS

Looks like we'll need a new member to fill his seat.

Then again, maybe no one will jump at the opportunity.

The crisis launched at 12:01 this morning. That's when every member of the Diamond Ring received a video at his personal email account. The tape should have been familiar—it's Klaus Herzog's murder. This time, though, the face of every onlooker is clearly visible, conveniently identified with name, address, and personal contact information for full internet distribution.

Every fucking member of the Diamond Ring is on the hook for aiding and abetting murder. Jonas and Ansel's demands are clear: Half a billion from every man, deposited to a Swiss bank account. If not received from every witness to the killing, the video will go public. They all sink or swim together.

This feels like fucking *Groundhog Day*. Alix and I received a similar threat last month, but on a much tighter timetable. I never had to make a final decision about ponying up; the cocksuckers released their tape in revenge for the raid I authorized on their Long Island compound.

This time, the Herzogs are fucking models of patience. They're giving the Ring six weeks to cough up the cash. I suspect that means they really want the money. They don't just want to ruin my clients' professional and business lives.

Wait.

One Diamond Ring tape has already been released.

Braiden Kelly's face is splashed across every news site in the world.

The Herzog motherfuckers are playing from their old rulebook. They *could* have jacked Kelly up for a billion dollars if they wanted, same as they tried with me. They could have gone for every kilo of Crash that Kelly lifted from the Philly warehouse. They could have pushed him out of the drug trade altogether, leaning on the Irish mob from Boston to Atlanta.

But they'd rather see him hang with Alix and me.

The headlines scream from my computer:

Philly Crime Boss Implicated in Freeport Murder

Blood on Kelly's Hands

Kelly Murder Tape Breaks Internet

Jonas and Ansel have their revenge for the warehouse raid. They've got it in fucking spades.

And they're smart sons of bitches too. Because every other member of the Diamond Ring has a front-row seat to what will happen if he doesn't pay up. The writing's on the fucking wall.

And Diamond Freeport's about to collapse under the weight of it all.

9

ALIX

I stand in the hospital waiting room, staring at an aquarium full of brightly colored fish. I'm trying to catch my breath after braving the mad crowd of paparazzi who followed me here to the hospital. I'm grateful the hyenas aren't allowed inside the building, but I'm already dreading the gauntlet when I leave.

I read somewhere that fishtanks are supposed to be soothing; that's why they keep them in places where people are under a lot of stress. Maybe that's true. But I keep thinking of all the movies I've watched where a massive aquarium is destroyed—usually by gunshot—and a tidal wave of fish and water drowns everything in sight.

I feel like I'm the one drowning here.

Jonas and Ansel Herzog are doing their level best to destroy me. Me, and everyone I've come to depend on—Trap and his Diamond Ring. I killed the Herzogs' brother so they're going to kill me, inch by painful inch.

I don't believe in heaven. I think the world we live in is actually hell. That's why we have war. Poverty. Disease. That's why men like the Herzogs exist, predators who consume women, children, anyone weaker than they are.

Hell is the only explanation for Klaus Herzog's "special guests," the men of power and prestige who brutalized me for personal pleasure.

Hell explains street drugs—Crash, meth, heroin.

Hell explains Leo.

For the first seventeen years of my life, I wasn't closer to anyone. For the next nine years, I ached for him. I prayed for him. I was desperate to save him.

And for the last three years I cursed him. He sold me to Herzog. He got himself killed, so I couldn't even beg him to save me, couldn't plead with him to help me escape. I couldn't hurt him the way he devastated me, couldn't kick him or scratch him or bite him.

The old Alix would have been overjoyed to discover her twin was still alive. No matter what he did, no matter how far he strayed, she would have hugged him and kissed his cheek and wept tears of joy that he'd somehow, miraculously been spared.

But the new Alix, the damned Alix, *me*... I can't rejoice. I can't celebrate. My heart has been replaced by a rock.

And the worst part? The most hellish fact of all?

I need to see him. I need to talk with him. I need to find out what he knows about Jonas and Ansel, what he can tell us about their movements, their plans, their secrets. That's the only way Trap can get to the brothers. Can kill them. Can set us free forever.

I turn my back on the aquarium and walk down the hall to my brother's private suite. This is a hospital, not a swank apartment building, but there's a heavy wooden door at the end of the hall. A doorbell is clearly labeled beside the shiny brass lever that takes the place of a doorknob: "Guests: Please ring bell for access during visiting hours."

Guest. That implies someone who's welcome. I'm pretty

sure Leo doesn't want to see me. So I ignore the bell. I palm the lever and step inside.

In some ways, this is clearly a hospital room. There's a dispenser of hand sanitizer just inside the door, beside a sink and a container for sharps. A computer screen displays constantly changing data—pulse rate, body temperature, blood pressure, respiratory rate, oxygen saturation. A matching panel on the far wall reports all the same data.

But the rest of the room looks like it belongs in an old-money mansion. The laminate floor resembles oak planks. Visitor chairs are upholstered in soft leather, made even more inviting by plush throw pillows. One wall is filled with a television the size of a football field, and a coffee table is covered with a tangle of gaming devices. Knick-knacks are scattered around the room—vases and carved wooden bowls, books and heavy stone bookends and a Waterford clock.

The bed is angled to face the floor-to-ceiling windows, with their view of the Delaware Bay. Standard hospital linens have been replaced with softly patterned sheets that look like they have a thread count in the low millions. A heavy wool blanket is folded across the foot of the bed, its plaid resembling a clan tartan.

But none of that can disguise the fact that the man in the bed is a patient.

Leo is dozing, sitting up against his pillows, wearing gray silk pajamas. He's been bathed and shaved, both his beard and his hair. The stubble on top of his head reveals bald patches and the curved lines of badly healed scars. His face looks like cheese that's been left too long in the sun—pale, pale, pale, and covered with a sheen of sweat.

A monitor in his breast pocket trails half a dozen wires. An IV line runs into the back of his bruised, bony hand. He moans as I step closer to the bed, and his fingers spasm on a plastic grip, his thumb pressing a dangerous-looking red button over and over again.

I must make some sound, because his eyes crack open. One of them is still caked with a greenish crust, and I wonder if he can see out of it. His mouth works and he looks like a baby bird, ravenous but helpless. "Alix," he croaks.

I'm supposed to say something. I'm supposed to help. But all I can do is stare at him like he's some sort of science experiment, like he's a film I'm watching in high school biology, something I have to memorize if I'm going to pass the test.

"More," he begs, giving the plastic grip a shake. "Need... More..."

I look at the IV hanging from a pole attached to the bed. The full bag is covered with writing, long chemical names that I don't understand. A drop falls from the bag to the tubing that snakes into Leo's hand.

"Please..." Leo says.

That's what Leo always says. Leo always begs.

And just like that, I'm back in Herzog's Holding Room. I'm strapped to the table. My head is filled with jet-black cobwebs. I'm trying to understand why I ache, why I'm freezing, why I'm lying stark naked beneath the flat white ceiling.

Leo's begging didn't help then. And it won't help now. I trust that the doctors Trap hired know what they're doing. I believe that the medicine flowing into Leo's hand must be helping.

So I ignore his pitiful whimper and pull a chair closer to the bed.

"I need some information," I say, clear and matter-of-fact, like I'm hiring an electrician or a plumber.

He blinks as if I've just spoken to him in Ancient Greek.

"Your old bosses have a video they've threatened to share. One that'll hurt a lot of my friends. I can't let that happen. So I need ammunition. Something I can use to keep them from acting. Something that will keep my friends safe."

This should be easy. Jonas and Ansel Herzog are drug lords. All I need is hard proof, and the feds will do the dirty work.

But Trap has had the finest minds he can hire working on

the problem for nearly three months. He's paid private investigators and security experts. Hackers and mercenaries.

The Herzogs have perfected their defenses over decades. They have shell corporations and silent partners, offshore bank accounts and asset protection trusts. Hundreds if not thousands of people wake every morning with the sole goal of keeping Jonas and Ansel Herzog's business dealings confidential.

But Leo's been on the inside. He must have seen some loose end, a tiny thread that Trap can grab onto. If any part of the cloth starts to unravel, there's hope.

"Leo!" I say, purposely sharpening my voice. "Let's start with the easy things. Did you always work in Philadelphia's Navy Yard?"

It takes him forever to answer. He hits the red plunger half a dozen times. He swallows hard and licks his chapped lips. But he finally shakes his head.

"Great!" I say. And once again, I'm awash in déjà vu. Leo and I are sitting at the kitchen table in Potomac, Maryland. Dad is working late at the office. Candace is taking her daughters, our stepsisters, out to dinner, but Leo and I aren't allowed to leave until we finish our homework.

I'm trying to get Leo to solve a polynomial equation. He's copied my homework for the first four weeks of the quarter, but mid-term exams are coming up, and he's going to fail if I can't get him to understand the concept. For the first time in all our tutoring sessions, he's finally figured out that he has to set the variable factor to zero. I'm so excited I start to laugh, and then Leo's laughing with me, and we're pounding the table and howling like maniacs. Candace, pouring herself another bourbon and ginger, edges past us like what we have might be contagious, which only makes us laugh harder.

No one's laughing now.

"Great," I say again. "Where were you before Philadelphia?"

"Narnia," he says.

Leo always loved Narnia. In our childhood games, he played Peter, and I played Lucy, a believer in magic till the end. Leo had a stuffed lion, because of his name, and we called it Aslan and made up elaborate stories.

But now I tell him, "You weren't in Narnia. Where were you before Philadelphia?"

"Narnia," he insists. "I went through the wardrobe. I met Mr. Tumnus."

His voice is high and reedy, like he can't quite catch his breath. His thumb has slowed down on the red button; he's rubbing it now, like it's some sort of worry stone.

I make one more try. "Narnia isn't real, Leo. Where—"

But he interrupts me. "It *is* real!"

"We read the books with Mom—"

"I've been there!

"You might have dreamed—"

"It's safe there! No one can hurt me there! The bad men can't go there!"

He's frantic now. His legs thrash beneath his sheets like he's determined to run all the way to his imaginary refuge. Two spots of color bloom high on his cheeks, and his breath comes in short, sharp pants.

"Leo—"

"I'm Peter!"

"You're not!" I say, filled with an anger I can't begin to control. "You're Leo Aidan Key. And you have to help me, right now. You owe me!"

He closes his eyes and covers his ears with his hands, like a toddler throwing a tantrum. He pulls his knees up to his chest. He starts to rock violently, humming to himself, a tuneless song I can't identify.

An alarm rings from the computer panel above the bed.

"Leo," I say, fighting to grab his hands.

His humming grows to a steady moan. He flings himself

back with enough strength that his skull bounces off the headboard.

"Leo!" I shout.

Before I can reach him, before I can calm him down, the door opens. A nurse rushes in, her white shoes squeaking on the floor that looks like wood. "Mr. Key," she says, planting beefy hands on Leo's shoulders. "Mr. Key!

She glances over her shoulder and snaps at me, "You have to leave now."

"I can't—"

"Now!" she commands.

"But he's my—"

She loosens her grip on Leo just long enough to hit a large square button on the computer display. "Security to Room 1201," she says.

I could wait. I could try to explain. I could stay in the hall until she gets Leo settled, until he stops that horrible, keening moan.

But I'm not strong enough for that. Not brave enough. I don't have enough faith—that Leo will stop, that he can tell me what I need, that he can ever be the brother I used to love.

So I hold up my hands as two armed security guards pound into the room. I keep my head high. I walk to the elevator like I own the entire hospital. And as I make my way to the parking garage, I wonder if anyone ever manages to break out of hell.

10

TRAP

I walk into Alix's office, hoping she has a minute to go over schedules before I head to Wilmington for the monthly Chamber of Commerce meeting. Clients are starting to hear about the incredible job she did auctioning Jim Farquhar's Monet. With the end of the calendar year approaching, three of my most valuable customers want to run their own sales. There's a suite of ten Warhol prints, each one a different endangered species. There's a Picasso nude from his Blue Period. And there's a bronze Rodin sculpture, a life-size version of his *Thinker*, cast while the sculptor was still alive.

I know jack shit about art. But I can plug words into Google. And the answers I'm getting say we're talking about fifty million dollars worth of art changing hands. And the freeport gets a cut of every deal.

I'm already entering her office as I knock on her door. So I'm perfectly situated to see her leap six feet in the air as surprise squeezes a bark from her throat. She slams down the cover of her laptop and plucks both buds from her ears.

"What are you watching?" I ask.

"Nothing," she answers, too quickly.

But *nothing* doesn't make a person breathe like they're wrapping up a marathon. *Nothing* doesn't make hands tremble. *Nothing* doesn't leave palms sweaty enough to cast ghost shadows on a desk blotter.

I'd think she was watching porn, but I know what Alix looks like when she's turned on. And the woman I'm keeping satisfied in bed doesn't need to watch made-up shit to get off.

"Bullshit," I say, closing her office door before I walk around behind her.

"Trap—"

I open the computer. A video is frozen on the screen—Alix in a latex cat-suit, triple-teamed by the fucking Herzog brothers. Her face is stretched into a scream that rips something open deep inside my gut.

"What the fuck?" I demand.

She closes the screen before she answers. Her motions are tight. Prim. Like she's the fucking schoolmarm in some Old West town. "I need to watch it."

She answers like that makes perfect sense. She needs to drink water. She needs to breathe air. She needs to watch those jizzwipes fuck her.

"The fuck you do."

"We need to get to them, Jonas and Ansel. We need to stop them before they release the Diamond Ring's names."

"*I* need to stop them."

"You said we're in this together."

Fuck. I did say that. But I argue, "I hire private investigators. I buy off hackers. I pay Sawgrass mercs to blast their way in. You don't wade through this shit anymore."

"I lived this shit," she says, and the word sounds dirtier because her mouth's so clean. "I lived it, and it's part of me, and

I'm never going to forget it. You can hire all the guys you want, but that hasn't worked so far. Men have *died* doing things your way. Now I have to try this. I have to fix this. I have to make it right."

"Princess—" I start.

"Don't say that."

"Alix," I try again, willing to choose my battles.

"I tried talking to Leo!" she says, like the words claw at her windpipe. "I went to the hospital, and I asked him for help, and he started babbling like a madman!"

Not for the first time, I wonder if I made the wrong decision on the Philadelphia docks. If Leo Fucking Key was rotting in the ground right now, Alix could finally begin moving on. Getting over his betrayal.

But I say, "He's got a long road ahead of him. He came in half-starved. He had Hep A, Hep B, and the clap. Load detox on top of that, not just withdrawal, but the hard shit, kicking the actual addiction… It's going to be a long time before Leo's able to talk to you."

"We don't have a long time! Jonas and Ansel are going after the Diamond Ring in five weeks! And you and I could be indicted any day! So could Braiden Kelly."

I hear the panic in her voice. I could shove aside that fucking computer and bend her over her desk. I could make her come three times in the next half hour and order her to suck me off by noon. I could keep us both here till midnight, until we're chafed and raw and half-dying of thirst.

But none of that's a long-term solution.

The long-term solution—one that'll last for years after the fucking—is to keep Alix's mind busy. To prove to her, over and over, how much she's worth.

And I remember a promise I made, one I kept private at the time. One I'm overdue on keeping.

"Let's go," I say.

"Go where?"

"You'll find out."

She laughs in disbelief. "You've got to be kidding."

"Clock's ticking," I say.

I watch her give in. "What do I need?"

"Nothing." And then I repeat, "Let's go."

She already has her phone in her pocket. And I let her grab her purse. But that's the only delay I permit before I text Susan Richards and tell her I'll be out of the office for the rest of the day. I also ask her to phone ahead, so Alix and I won't completely surprise the man we're going to meet.

11

ALIX

The crowd moving around me doesn't seem to notice the ten-foot-tall live flower displays. Not a leaf or petal is out of place. I wonder how often the forest of red and orange and yellow has to be replaced. Maybe the florists work at midnight, so no one ever sees their magic.

"Ready?" Trap asks.

I look past the flowers to a gigantic staircase—the height of four stories and wide enough for an army to march shoulder to shoulder. "Don't we need tickets?"

"Not for this," Trap says and leads the way across the lobby.

I've never been to the Metropolitan Museum of Art before. I've read about it in books. Seen pictures. But my mother died before she could take Leo and me to New York. Candace likes the city more for shopping than museums, although she follows the Met Gala every year like she's some sort of apprentice fashion reporter.

I'm already thinking about the treasures in this building—

Impressionist paintings and Egyptian mummies and Tiffany stained-glass windows. Trap and I made good time driving up from Dover, but the museum closes at five, according to a sign at the entrance. We'll be rushed, trying to take it all in.

And it's only a matter of time before someone recognizes us. Maybe they'll be polite enough to fake selfies with us in the background. But chances are, they'll follow us from room to room, video cameras rolling. That's what happens at the grocery store, at the gas station, any time Trap and I dare to leave the confines of the freeport.

But for now, Trap leads the way, and I follow like a dazed little lamb. We pass through a giant doorway and I stop dead, like I've forgotten how to walk.

Books.

I'm surrounded by books. They stretch on, room after room. They're stacked on giant waist-high tables. They line floor-to-ceiling shelves.

There are hand-size pamphlets. There are coffee-table books the size of a suitcase. There are series covering dozens of artists, and there are ten-volume sets doing deep dives on individual painters and sculptors. Some covers are in black and white. Others are in eye-searing color.

Everywhere I look, there's something I long to read. In fact, when I step closer to a shelf labeled European Painting 16th Century, I see some old familiar friends. There's Mona Lisa's mysterious smile fronting a three-volume set on Leonardo da Vinci. God and Adam sprawl across a gigantic book about the Sistine Chapel. A pretty Madonna holds a squirming child on a paperback about Raphael.

I know these books. I read them in Herzog's mansion. I sorted them in one insane flurry of a day—with the help of his other slaves—to meet his heartless deadline. Looking around, I feel like I'm surrounded by family.

"Do you mind if I take a few minutes?" I ask Trap.

"Take all the time you want. That's why we're here."

"I might buy a few," I warn him.

"We're buying everything."

I laugh, because that's such a Trap thing to say. I pick up a canvas basket to hold my selections. "Here," I order him as I make my first choice, a huge book on Michelangelo's sculpted slaves. "Put your big muscles to work."

He refuses to take the basket. "I'm going to need my hands free."

I know exactly what he can do with those hands. "Not here," I whisper, pretending to study a book about virgin saints. I can feel myself blushing, and Trap starts to laugh.

"You, Princess, have got a dirty mind."

I'm still protesting when a tall, thin man approaches. He's wearing a brown pin-stripe suit that matches the thinning hair combed across his scalp. His bifocals have slipped low on his nose, and his burgundy tie is just slightly askew.

"Mr. Prince," he says. "My apologies for keeping you waiting."

"No apology necessary," Trap says. I wonder if Ichabod Crane catches the way Trap tightens his jaw as they shake hands. I wait for the familiar five-point release as Trap taps his index finger against the nearest book. His voice is almost easy as he says, "I don't believe you've met my Fine Arts Specialist at the freeport. Martin Updike. Alix Key." And then, for my benefit, he adds, "Martin manages all of the Met's stores."

It's easy for me to shake hands; I don't mind the physical contact. I just have to bite back a grin at the name of my job. Trap dreamed it up when he gave me my freeport employee lanyard, and I'm still not used to the title.

After Mr. Updike and I have murmured how pleased we are to meet each other, the tall man practically bows in front of Trap. "I hope I'm not being too presumptuous," he says. "But I've taken the liberty of creating a new holiday card with the Bellini we acquired through your generous donation last year. Of course, the design will be exclusive for your use, as long as you desire. I must admit, I didn't expect to have the privilege of showing it to you in person."

Bellini—a Venetian master who painted in the fifteenth century. I can't imagine how much Trap donated to the museum for them to buy such a treasure. But he's explained it to me before. He needs the tax write-off. And with any luck, he'll land new freeport clients from among his fellow donors.

Still, a Renaissance masterpiece? And an exclusive holiday card to send the freeport's season's greetings? I'm impressed.

"I'm sure the card will be perfect," Trap says. "My assistant will follow up with you next week. But Alix and I are here today for a different reason."

Mr. Updike stands a little taller. His eyes narrow behind his tilted glasses. He looks like a giraffe studying the horizon for the choicest trees to harvest. "Of course," he says. "Anything I can do to help."

Trap looks at me. The corners of his mouth are turned up in the slightest of smiles. I can see the fire stirring in his eyes. "We'd like to buy your books," he says.

Mr. Updike waits for the rest of the sentence. Books about Bellini... Books about Venice... Books about Renaissance painting... When Trap doesn't say more, Mr. Updike clears his throat. "Our books," he says. "Which ones would you like?"

"All of them."

"Excuse me?"

"All of them," Trap repeats. "We're building an art history library at Diamond Freeport to support Alix in her job. And we need one copy of every book you have in the museum."

12

TRAP

I'll give Updike credit. It only takes him a moment to hide his astonishment. He clears his throat like he's trying to cover up the sound of a fart. "Our entire collection. We can certainly do that," he says, like I've asked for an extra bookmark.

"Excellent." I look at Alix. She's staring at me like I've lost my fucking mind.

"Obviously, we can't strip our stores down to bare shelves today," Updike says.

Obviously.

"Might I suggest that we start by drawing up a list of our complete inventory? Our acquisitions clerk can organize it by publisher, to expedite the purchase process. I assume you intend to take delivery at the freeport?"

"You assume correctly."

"An order this size…" I see that he's starting to recognize the reality of my request.

I'm the single largest donor the Met has seen in fifty years.

They'll do just about anything to kiss my ass. If I asked for a list of the bookstore's inventory, they'd give it to me. Hand-deliver the information to Dover, if that's what I said I needed.

But I'm not buying direct from publishers. I'm not skipping the middleman. I'm making my purchase *through the museum.* They'll turn a profit on every single book—probably a wider margin than usual, because the publishers will cream their pants to fulfill a purchase like this.

"An order this size," Updike tries again. "There will be certain logistics… I want everything to flow as smoothly as possible… Certainly you don't mind if I consult with my manager in charge of acquisitions?"

"I don't mind at all," I say. "Alix and I can go explore the museum. We'll check back at close of business today?"

Okay. I'm being an ass. The museum's only open for two more hours. But the bill of sale will end up topping seven figures. Maybe eight. Martin Updike can scramble a little.

Because the look on Alix's face makes it all worthwhile.

Updike murmurs something about getting a curator to show us around. I start to refuse—there's no reason we can't read the write-ups on the wall like every other visitor to the museum. But Alix's eyes look like Christmas ornaments when Updike makes the suggestion. Makes sense—she wants to share notes with an expert, not some barbarian like me.

"That would be excellent," I say. Updike excuses himself to make some calls, promising to be back in a few minutes.

Alix waits until he's out of earshot before she says, "You're insane."

I grin. "How can you say that?"

"We don't need all these books!"

"I do."

"What are you going to do with them?"

"Make you happy."

She wasn't expecting that. She opens her mouth. Closes it. Opens it again and draws a breath, but her eyes have gone all shiny. Finally she says, "You don't have to buy an entire library to make me happy. You already do that, every single day."

"Maybe I have an ulterior motive."

"Like what?"

"Like making you grateful. So I can have my wicked way with you."

She doesn't smile. Instead she answers like she's making a solemn vow. "You can have your wicked way with me any time you choose. Any place. Any way."

"Careful, Princess. Don't make promises you aren't willing to keep."

"Who says I'm not willing?"

Before I can think of a way to test her in this very public museum, I hear someone clearing their throat. I turn around to find a harried looking woman. The walkie-talkie strapped to her hip squawks, and she automatically reaches down to adjust the volume.

"Mr. Prince?" she asks. "Ms. Key? My name is Kellen Nolan. Mr. Updike asked me to show you around the highlights of our collection. He says we have a couple of hours."

I'm wondering why Updike chose Kellen as our guide. She's about Alix's age. Dressed all in black. Her hair is in a messy ponytail, and she has gauges in both ears. She looks like she's auditioning for some foreign movie where everyone drinks Campari and smokes skinny cigarettes.

"That's right," I say.

Kellen turns to Alix. "Do you have any preference about where you'd like to start?"

Alix answers without hesitation. "The Impressionists, please."

Kellen beams. "My favorite. Right this way."

She leads us to a bank of elevators labeled *Employees Only*. By the time we reach the second floor, we know she got her PhD in art history from Yale, and she's studied at the Sorbonne in Paris. She wrote her dissertation on a guy I've never heard of, and she's been working at the Met for three and a half years.

But none of that is why Updike chose her. Updike chose her because Kellen focuses on Alix like my princess is her private patron, her fellow student, and her long-lost best friend, all rolled up in one.

Alix does her best to fold me into the conversation. But I don't give a shit about unblended color, natural light, and the ambivalence of spatial imprecision. I pretend like I'm interested in a painting of some woman with bare tits, holding a bowl of orange fruit, but I'm really watching Alix shine.

We finish with the Impressionists, and the crowd starts to thin. Kellen takes us to her favorite medieval altarpiece. That's quickly followed by her favorite marble statue, her favorite daguerreotype portrait, and her favorite Lalique necklace.

Alix eats it up, every bite. She asks questions, sponges up the answers, and races off for more before I've even figured out what I'm supposed to be looking at. I've never seen her this relaxed, this *on*, at least outside of our bedroom.

Kellen says, "Let me take you to the Temple of Dendur." Along the way, she explains that it's an ancient Egyptian temple. The huge sandstone blocks were transported to the museum before the temple's original valley was flooded by a new dam. The entire thing has been rebuilt in a gigantic glass-walled gallery.

"This is one of the rooms for the Met Gala," Kellen says. Before she can go on, though, her walkie-talkie spits out a burst of static. "Excuse me," Kellen says. "I'm afraid I have to take this."

She fiddles with the volume and speaks into the device. I can barely make out the reply, but it must not be good news. Kellen frowns and holds up a finger in the universal sign that she'll just be a minute. She waves her hand, inviting us to look around without her.

Alix and I climb the steps to the temple, giving our guide a little privacy to resolve whatever problem she's dealing with.

"Thank you," Alix says as we walk into the sandstone structure.

"For what?"

"For all of this."

I squint at the carvings on the walls around us. "For a couple of palm trees and a guy with the head of a jackal?"

She plants her hands on my chest. "Seriously. I love you."

"I love you too." It's not the first time we've said it to each other. But it's the first time the words have just fallen out like that, easy and balanced and light.

She turns her face up, and I brush a kiss against her lips. It's not supposed to mean anything. We're in a goddamn Egyptian temple, for fuck's sake. But Alix's fingers tighten on my shirt, pulling me closer. She opens her mouth, and her sly, hot tongue slips against mine.

When Alix sighs, I'm instantly as hard as good old Pharaoh's sandstone tomb. I shift my feet for better balance and slip my hand past the waistband of her jeans, fully aware of the fact that Kellen Nolan is just the other side of the temple's solid walls.

13

ALIX

I buck when Trap's fingers slide past my panties to brush my clit, and I let out a little shriek of surprise. "Hush," he whispers against my lips. "You're in a fucking museum."

I laugh, until his free hand slides inside the collar of my shirt. He pinches my nipple, hard enough to make me squeak again. At the same time, he curls a finger deep inside my pussy. "Trap," I moan.

"Quiet. Or the security guards will throw us out."

This is what he promised. Trap is having his wicked way with me. He's igniting every nerve ending in my body because he's chosen this place, this time, and I'll be mortified if we're discovered by random tourists or Kellen or her boss.

I bury my face in Trap's right shoulder, taking care to avoid the stitches in his left. If I hurt him, he doesn't give any sign. Instead, he refines his approach between my thighs, rubbing my clit with his thumb as he fills me with two smart fingers.

We're making out like horny kids, hiding on a school field

trip. I start humping his hand, rocking back and forth to find the perfect pressure against his wrist. I lean back just enough to stroke him through his jeans, feeling his cock grow heavy and hard.

I shift my feet, giving him a better angle to drive deep. At the same time, I work his zipper, sliding my fingers past the metal teeth. I slip through the fly of his boxers and run a single fingernail down the length of his twitching cock.

"Fuck," he grunts, but I purse my lips, silently reminding him to *shhhhh.* I close my fingers around his cock, squeezing hard enough to make him huff.

He wastes no time getting his revenge. He shifts his slick fingers to my clit, pinching slowly, tighter, tighter, ratcheting me close to the edge of pain. I catch my breath, the better to measure the frantic fire sizzling beneath his grip.

Just when I think I have to stop him, or maybe I only need to slow him down a bit, he releases the throbbing nub. I gasp. I have to. And then he's got three fingers pressing into my pussy, hooking me at an impossible angle.

Pinch. Plunge. Pinch. Plunge.

I've given up on teasing his cock. I'm clutching his good shoulder with one hand, trying to hold steady. I've got the back of my right hand pressed against my mouth, pushing back all the words I want to shout.

Pinch.

Plunge.

His lips open. His tongue pushes the back of his lower teeth. I can see the letter C; I can feel it in my bones. He's about to give me permission to come.

And we're frozen by a blast of static.

It's coming from the other side of the ancient monument, transferring through two feet of stone. But Kellen's voice rings loud and clear. "Alix? Mr. Prince? Sorry about that."

Trap's hand leaves me so fast I stagger. His grin is twisted as he mouths a word: "Sorry."

He fixes his zipper with his clean hand, shoving the other in his pocket. "No problem," he calls to Kellen. He turns and heads back to the temple's entrance. "Alix and I could spend all day looking at this."

I'm flushed and flustered, unsteady on my feet. I force myself to take a deep breath, to hold it for a count of five, to exhale slowly, until my lungs are completely empty.

Trap, meanwhile, is talking on the other side of the wall. "Are those photographs of the original setting?" he asks our unwitting guide.

"Yes. You can see how the temple was oriented to the river…" Kellen's voice grows more distant, and I know Trap has led her away to give me another moment to recover.

What is it about this man? Why is my body locked into his orbit?

I love you too.

He said it, as easily as I did. The words mean more than his fingers. More than his fortune. More than his glibly occupying Kellen while I remember how to breathe and walk and act like a normal human being.

I run my fingers through my hair. I look down to make sure my clothes won't betray me. And I step out of the temple to finish my tour of the greatest museum in the world.

14

TRAP

~

I've slept eight hours, showered, and shaved, but I swear to God I can still smell Alix on my fingers as I pull up a chair to my lawyer's boardroom table.

I can't. Not really. The same way I can't actually hear her chanting my name when I finally let her come last night, pressed against the penthouse window, forty floors above Central Park. The same way I'm not picturing her mouth stretched into a perfect O as she holds her breath and shatters.

"Ms. Key. Mr. Prince."

Fuck. Time to pay attention, which would be a lot easier to do if Alix wasn't sitting right beside me.

Campbell J. Throckmorton III is the best criminal lawyer money can buy. He doesn't bother with one of those massive New York law firms. Instead, he keeps a dozen associates on hand to do his exclusive bidding, along with a supporting staff of twenty-five—private investigators, accountants, the works. His name is almost as well-known as his clients' and the last time he lost a case was when that Oscar-Award-winning actor lied about driving his Lamborghini into Lake Pontchartrain with the two whores he picked up on Bourbon Street.

"Throck" wears French cuffs, diamond cufflinks, and a multi-color bowtie. His shoes probably cost more than any suit I've ever owned, and I bet I could buy a loaded computer for what he spent on his last haircut. The table we're sitting at seats twenty and easily covers eighty square feet. With Manhattan rent running a hundred bucks a foot, he's paying eight grand a month for a fucking table.

Throck inclines his head toward Alix. "Ms. Key. It's always a…pleasure to see you…. If you wouldn't…mind stepping out to the lobby…one of my associates will be…happy to get you a cup of coffee."

"She's here with me," I say, ignoring the long pauses Throck inserts every few words. I'm paying this shark two thousand bucks an hour, and he's stretching for every penny.

"Of course," Throck says. But then, to Alix: "Ms. Key." He looks toward the door with a pointed nod of his head.

"I don't have anything to hide from her," I say.

"I appreciate that," Throck says. "But if a third party is… present while you and I talk…Mr. Prince, then your attorney-client privilege can be…challenged in a court of law. In the interest of…preserving that valuable right…I'm afraid I must insist that Ms. Key…wait for you outside this room."

She leaves. The second the door closes behind her, the stitches in my left shoulder start to burn. I make a fist to keep from scratching at the healing wound. I can't imagine what Throck would say if he found out how I got shot.

I clear my throat. "I appreciate your making time to meet with us. With me. As long as we were already in New York, I figured we should do this face-to-face."

"Of course," Throck says and then he pauses for so long I wonder if it's my turn to talk again. But he finally continues: "I just wish I had a more…complete update about the status of your case."

"Any update at all is good with me. Most of what I know about criminal law I learned on TV."

"Yes, well…" Another one of those endless pauses. "We tend not to…have sex in elevators…as much as our onscreen brethren."

I flash on the thought of pushing Alix up against an elevator wall. What the fuck is wrong with me?

I force myself to laugh at his little joke. "I know that on TV, they need to wrap up all the drama in an hour. But frankly, I'm confused by the pace of this case. The cops raided my house four weeks ago. The same day, they interviewed Alix and me. They sweated her for hours. But we haven't heard a word since."

"On TV," Throck preaches, "the investigators…only work one case. They maintain an entire lab…dedicated to catching one bad guy…. They can run any test they desire with near… instantaneous results."

"And in the real world?"

"In the real world…things take time…. Weeks to get DNA results."

"Whose DNA are they testing?"

"The alleged victim…. The brothers Herzog have certainly…cooperated by providing samples of their brother's DNA…. The police are comparing those findings to…samples from the alleged crime scene."

From my fucking dining room.

Which was stripped to the studs to destroy every last molecule of incriminating evidence. Trying to look like an innocent man, I stare my lawyer straight in the eye and lie. "But the entire fu— freaking video was a hoax. Some sort of deep fake. Artificial intelligence. There was never any DNA to sample."

"That's certainly our…primary defense at the moment."

I bull forward. "That's been our primary defense for the past month. What I want to know is whether the prosecutor is buying it."

"We've had...preliminary discussions."

I'm tempted to take out my wallet and count out a stack of hundreds, slam them on the table, and demand that this guy start speaking at a normal pace. Instead, I force myself to ask, "What's been the substance of those preliminary discussions?"

"I've explained our...theory of the case. Ms. Rodriguez has explained that she...disagrees."

"Why does *she* have a bug up her—" I pretend to cough while I figure out a way to rephrase my question that's fit for polite society. "Why is she so intent on making this case?"

"Ms. Rodriguez is an...up and coming star in...the District Attorney's office. She wants to...make her name. And your case...for better or worse...is generating a lot of press."

"That's exactly why Alix and I want to get this behind us."

Throck spreads his hands like he's dealing five card stud in slow motion. "Yet another example...I'm afraid...of where our interests differ from...the District Attorney's."

Of course he doesn't say "DA." District Attorney is three syllables longer. I push a little harder. "Have you spoken with those experts I gave you?" I got three good names from Cole Wolf, one of my freeport clients. He guaranteed they'd be solid on the witness stand, every one of them capable of explaining deep fakes to a newborn.

"All in good time... All in good time."

"When you say Rodriguez 'disagrees', what does that mean? That she has some sort of evidence against us? She can prove it isn't a deep fake?"

"Lawyers have been...relying on DNA evidence for...forty years.... We've relied on video authentication for...half that.... We lawyers are a...suspicious bunch.... Ms. Rodriguez is... biding her time."

"So what am I supposed to do while we're waiting? What can I do to make sure we wrap up a trial this year?"

Throck's laugh is a deep hooting sound, like a foghorn blowing underwater. "This year? We may be…years away from trial."

If I have to listen to this slow-motion mouthpiece for years, I might slash my own goddamn throat. "Then what? What can we do now?"

"You and Ms. Key can…check your memories for…contradictions…. Make sure the facts are…clear in your own minds…. All the facts…. Not just the night of the…alleged murder…. But from the…moment you met."

"That's all?" I ask, because that's what I think an innocent guy would say. "Because Alix and I don't have anything to hide about how we met."

And that's the truth. We're both ready to swear—the truth, the whole truth, and nothing but the truth—about hooking up at Debasement. It's the three years after that night where we plan to take a few liberties.

"That's all," Throck says. He climbs to his feet with the careful deliberation of a grizzly waking from hibernation. "Please try not to…worry, Mr. Prince…. These things take…time."

I want the guy to trust me, so I have to shake his hand. After, my desire to punch my fist through the nearest wall has nothing to do with the Beast inside my head.

I want to protect Alix.

I want to make this case go away.

But I just spent two grand to find out that's not happening any time soon.

15

ALIX

"You're looking better," I say to Leo.

And after almost two weeks in the hospital, he is. He's sitting in one of the leather chairs. He still has an IV but it runs automatically; he isn't clutching the plastic grip like it's the only thing keeping him from drowning. His eye looks clear, and his lips aren't as chapped.

According to Trap, they're keeping him for one more week. They'll monitor his heart, making sure he stays stable as the receptors in his brain are washed clean of the last remnants of Crash.

"I brought you some flowers," I say, handing him a bunch of daisies. I realized in the gift shop downstairs that I don't have a clue what type of flowers he likes. Maybe it's stupid getting a guy flowers, anyway. I just want him to know I care.

At least, I think I do. Maybe I just want him to answer my questions.

"Thanks," he says. He puts the daisies on the table beside his chair. I'm pretty sure he's forgotten them by the time his hand falls back in his lap.

He's staring out the window, like there's something fascinating on the bay. It's raining, though, and the sky is the same color as the water. The first hints of autumn color are washed out by the storm. Everything looks gray.

I should think of something fun to talk about. Come up with a childhood memory. Maybe a secret we shared.

But I'm not here because I want to get all chummy with my brother. Part of me still longs to see him chained to a table in the freeport warehouse.

I chickened out on that plan. But I'm not going to give up on getting what I want. What I need.

"Do you remember what we talked about the last time I was here?" I ask.

Leo shakes his head. "Everything's pretty foggy."

"I asked you about where you lived before you got to the warehouse in Philadelphia."

Every muscle in his body turns to steel. I remember when we were seven, and he brought me his Slinky, the metal rings twisted into a hopeless knot. "How did you do this?" I asked, truly astonished.

"I was just playing."

"Well, what do you want *me* to do with it?"

"You're a girl."

"Yeah."

"Well girls are better at fixing Slinkies than boys are."

"Who said *that*?"

"Everyone knows it's true."

I had no idea where he got such a stupid idea, but I took his toy. I ran the coils through my hands. I took the time to smooth out every twist. And by the time I got to the end, the Slinky was as good as new.

"See?" he said. "I knew you could fix it."

I want to fix things now. I want to make everything better. But I can't do it by myself. I can't do it if he doesn't share what he knows.

"I know this is scary," I say.

"Scary is what you call a ghost story when you're a kid."

"I wouldn't ask if it wasn't important."

"You would, if you didn't realize what might happen."

He's trying to protect me. My broken, half-dead brother is trying to keep me safe. Maybe I should appreciate his effort. But the truth is, he makes me want to scream.

"You do realize I've met Jonas and Ansel before?" I ask.

He twitches like a bird getting ready to fly from its nest.

That means I have to continue. "They came to Klaus's house. The house where you left me. The house where I was a slave."

He folds his arms around his belly like he's trying to disappear. I know how it feels, to want to hide like that. To try to escape.

"Klaus gave me to them, Leo. He dosed me with Crash and let them do whatever they wanted to me. You understand what that means, don't you? They hurt me. They hurt me bad enough that I was in a hospital bed for weeks. A hospital bed where I was a prisoner, not some cushy hideaway like this."

He starts to rock back and forth. I know I should pity a man who's been broken so thoroughly. But his very vulnerability lights a vengeful fire inside me.

"You're safe now," I say. "No one can get you. You've got doctors and nurses working to make you better. You've got Trap pouring thousands of dollars into getting your health back. Even if you don't give a crap about me, I'd think you'd want to do *something* to thank Trap."

He shakes his head, fast, like a dog drying off after a rainstorm.

"Use your words, Leo."

He just closes his eyes and hunches his shoulders.

"Dammit! I'm not asking you to *talk* to the Herzogs. You don't ever have to see them again. Just tell me where they kept you. Tell me who watched over you. Tell me how they're running their business, who they bought off to avoid the law, what they fucking eat for breakfast!"

Leo's eyes pop open. He stares at me like I just burst into flame. I never used to swear.

He doesn't have a clue how the past three years have changed me. How Trap has changed me. He doesn't know who I am.

"Poached eggs," he says. "With four triangles of toast. Butter. No jam."

He's actually telling me what those monsters ate. All the things I need to know, and he's reciting a stupid menu.

"What about the rest?" I push.

His mouth snaps closed. I remember when we first took swimming lessons, how we'd both gulp the biggest breaths we could and fight to stay under water the longest. No matter how hard I tried, Leo always won. I'd gasp at the surface, spitting out chlorine until he drifted up to join me, his smile as wide as the sun.

"Tell me, goddammit! How can we get at Jonas and Ansel Herzog?"

"That's just it," Leo says, and his voice is as calm as I've ever heard him. His face is smooth. His eyes are clear. "You can't. No one can get to the Herzogs. No one can go after them. *They* come after you. And there's nothing you can do about that."

For just a moment, I picture my brother strapped to the table I installed in my freeport gallery. I hear him pleading for hours, for days, for weeks. I smell his sweat and his piss and his shit, fermented for months.

But that never happened. It was my own sweat I smelled, in

Klaus Herzog's Holding Room. My own piss. My own shit. I was the one strapped to the table, helpless and pleading, because Leo put me there.

I leave the hospital before I give in to the urge to slap my brother blind.

16

TRAP

Yesterday's rain was the leading edge of a cold front—welcome to fucking October. My breath fogs as I cross the parking lot, heading home after a working Saturday. I've been thinking about what Throck said, about how Alix and I need to get our stories straight.

I have an idea.

Alix is out on the patio when I come in. She's tucked into one of the chaise lounges, with a blanket pulled up to her chin. She's got her arms wrapped around a giant stuffed panda, a prize I won for her at the county fair back in August, and she's watching something on her computer.

She looks like a kid, maybe half her age. She went to see Leo yesterday. I don't know what happened, but she barely said ten words to me all evening. She got up in the middle of the night and went to sleep in the guest room.

Fucking Leo Key.

I'm ready to cut off the freeloading cocksucker. Turn him

out of his hospital room and put him back on the streets. He's making Alix feel like shit, and he sure as hell isn't getting us any closer to dealing with the Herzogs before their goddamn blackmail deadline.

But when he goes back to Crash, or meth, or heroin, or whatever other poison he wants to pump into his veins, he's going to die. And I think that'll hurt Alix more.

Fucking, fucking Leo Key.

I slide open the glass door. And that's when I hear it: "Thank you, Daddy. Thank you for my pony."

It's Alix's voice, but it isn't. It's Alix, pretending to be a little girl. It's Alix, flirting like a cheap whore, fawning over a man who's telling her to suck his big fat cock.

The growl that rips from my throat is a lot more animal than human. I don't even realize I've made a noise until Alix slams shut the screen on her computer.

"Hi!" she says, sounding perfectly normal. "I didn't realize you were home."

I see scarlet.

Those videos broke her. The things Herzog made her do destroyed her will. He raped her mind.

I can't begin to fathom why she's watching that shit. But even more than that, I don't know how she can shut off her computer and greet me like everything's okay.

Nothing's okay. Nothing will ever be okay until I destroy the Herzogs. Get rid of them before they follow through on their threat to ruin the Diamond Ring.

But if I say that out loud, if I tell her what I'm thinking, if I let her know how many minutes of how many hours of every fucking day I think about getting revenge for what they did to her…

She'll think I'm judging her. Think that all of this is her fault.

So I play the game. I sit on the end of the chaise. I pull her feet onto my lap and I tuck the blanket back in to keep her warm and I pretend she wasn't just watching the video proof of the worst three years of her life.

"So here's an idea," I say.

"Yes?" Her chin rests on top of the panda's black-and-white head. I feel like a pervert for even thinking what I'm about to say.

"I thought we might drive over to the train station."

"Where do you want to go?"

She sounds confused. Which makes sense, because I've got a Lear jet, a Sikorsky helicopter, and a dozen high-performance cars at my disposal. A random train trip on the Northeast Corridor isn't my usual idea of fun.

"Throck said we need to make sure our stories are straight," I say.

"You told him what we made up?" She sounds shocked.

I shake my head. "We didn't talk specifics."

"But you and I both know the story."

We do. She and I met at Debasement and hooked up for one night. Went our separate ways. Things got rough for her, and she started turning tricks at the train station. After one especially bad day at the freeport, I was looking for something quick, something dirty, and I decided to pick up a girlfriend for the night. We were both shocked as hell to meet again after three long years.

I say, "I figure it can't hurt to pin down a few details. You know. The type of things we'd only notice if it had actually happened."

"If our story is too polished, it'll sound like a lie," she says.

"I'm not talking about polish. Just a couple of details for me to say. A couple for you. Specifics."

"What about the paps out front?"

Fucking paparazzi. But I've had a trick up my sleeve for a while, one I've been longing to try. "I'll have one of the security guys take out the Mercedes. He can drive over to the airfield, and they'll follow like fucking vultures."

We'll only be able to play that game once. But the dark windows of the luxury limo should buy us some privacy for tonight.

"Okay," she says, clearly unsure. "If you think we need to."

"Good girl," I say.

And just like that, the trip becomes something else.

We aren't two criminals, brushing up our alibi. Instead, she's my good girl. My princess. The woman who can only come when I give her permission.

She puts the panda on the flagstones beside her. She pushes the blanket down to her waist. She shivers in the cold air, just a little, and even in the dark, I can see the shadows of her rock-hard nips.

"If we're making this realistic," she says, "what should I wear?"

My throat goes dry, but I answer: "Your black bra, the one with the red flowers. That short little denim skirt. And your black stilettos. The ones with the crystal heels."

She laughs. "You're predictable."

"You have a problem with that?" I actually want to know.

"Not at all." She gets to the sliding door before she turns back. "Which panties should I wear?"

"None," I say.

She laughs again. "Predictable."

She takes one more step before she turns back. "Aren't you going to change?"

"Into what?"

Her eyes gleam. "Your tux," she says. "Diamond studs. Plain black braces."

"Your wish is my command," I say.

"The hell it is. You'll be the one issuing commands. Or I might as well stay home tonight."

I raise my eyebrows at the challenge. "Get dressed," I say. "Meet me in the garage in fifteen minutes. And bring the handcuffs from my dresser drawer."

17

ALIX

I stand on the corner outside the train station, wondering if anyone has ever actually lost a nipple to frostbite. A nipple, or some other sensitive body part equally vulnerable to the cold… I shouldn't have let Trap tell me what to wear. I should have dressed in an Arctic parka. With leggings and a heavy wool sweater. And long underwear underneath.

The ridiculous thing is, it was my idea for me to stand outside. According to our story, this is where I picked up dates.

How long can it take for Trap to drive around the block? It feels like he dropped me off hours ago. I slide my phone out of my bra and take a peek at the brightly lit screen.

Two minutes.

I've been standing outside the train station for only two minutes.

Trap's Hummer pulls around the corner. He slows down as he approaches the curb, lowering the window on the passenger side.

I hide my phone away and step up to the gigantic car. It's the largest vehicle in his garage, which makes it perfect for the game we're playing.

"Hey," I say, leaning forward to meet his gaze. I make a point of pressing my arms close to my sides, making my breasts test the limits of my lacy black bra. "Looking for a date?"

"I was hoping to find some company tonight." The words sound like he's dragging them over gravel. His white pleated shirt practically glows in the dark. He leans across and opens the passenger door. "Maybe you have a room somewhere? I can drive you home."

I shake my head. "My roommate sleeps pretty light. I don't want to wake her up." I pretend to think for a moment, and then I give him my biggest fake smile. "But I've never seen a car like this before. It looks like it has a really big engine."

He smirks. "Let me show you what it can do."

I step off the curb and into the car. As I close the door, I wonder about women who really do this kind of work. What sort of nerve does it take to drive off with strangers? How scary is it to leave behind the relative safety of a well-lit train station, of waiting passengers, of help just a quick shout away?

"I don't usually do this kind of thing," I say, getting back to the game.

"Pretty girl like you," Trap plays along. "It could be dangerous, out late at night. You're lucky a nice guy like me came along."

I fiddle with the hem of my skirt, raising it an inch or two. "About time something good happened to me. I just found out my landlord raised my rent. I'm going to end up a little short this month."

If Trap appreciates my improvisation, he keeps it to himself. "How short?"

"Two hundred bucks," I say. "But for extras, I'll need four."

"Extras?" he asks, his voice dropping a few notes.

I look up at him through my eyelashes. So much for sly

suggestions; it's time for hard-core negotiation. "You know," I say. "Like the movies. Deep throat. Doggy style. You can come on my face or my tits."

"What if I'm looking for something a little rougher than that?"

"I don't do rough. Not if I don't know my date."

"I can make it worth your while. Six hundred, and you let me use handcuffs."

I pretend like I'm thinking. "Eight. And you keep the key where I can see it."

He takes out his money clip and counts out eight crisp hundred-dollar bills. I try not to grab them, waiting until he's back on his side of the car before I tuck them into my bra.

I look back at the brightly lit entrance to the train station. "This time of night, the cops come around once an hour or so. Maybe you can drive us somewhere a little quieter?"

He doesn't say a word. Just keys the ignition and puts the car in gear.

I don't know where I thought he'd take me. It doesn't make sense to go back to the house—he'd never invite an actual hooker past the freeport gates. We could go to a hotel; money's no object. But that would leave a record, a charge on his credit card or a night manager who might inconveniently remember a rare cash transaction.

We can't do anything the police can't confirm as they follow up their investigation. So I shouldn't be surprised when he drives us to a shady part of town. He seems to choose an alley at random, but I bet he's done some research. He parks in the shadow of a massive black dumpster. After the headlights switch off, it's very dark in the car.

"You look a little cold," he says. "Maybe I can help you warm up, if you come sit over here?"

As I unfasten my seatbelt, he reclines his seat. It's easier than I think it will be to climb across the console. His hands steady my hips as I straddle his legs. "Mmm," I say, like I'm getting my first taste of my favorite flavor of ice cream. "This *is* better."

Thinking ahead, I slide my hands under his black braces. The space is tight, but he sits up enough to give me room to slide those suspenders from his shoulders. While I'm at it, I work the diamond studs on his shirt. The cotton falls to either side, exposing the hard muscles of his chest and abs.

I can just make out the shadow of the stitches on his left shoulder. I want to lean down. I want to kiss them. I want to make them better.

But the erection tenting his pants is too big to ignore. The close quarters make it a challenge to work his zipper, but I manage. I reach inside his trousers, through the fly of his silk boxers. I grasp him firmly, stroking hard. There's already a slick of moisture waiting for me at the tip. He grits his teeth as I spread the bead with my thumb.

"I paid for the porn star experience," he says.

I'm surprised to feel my cheeks flush. There's nothing I promised for those extra six hundred bucks that I haven't given him for free before. But I tap the center of his chest and say, "Patience, big boy."

His growl simmers down as I work the button on his pants. We both have to shift from side to side a few times, but I'm rewarded with his gorgeous cock standing at full attention, unbound by the tux I made him wear.

My hum of appreciation is genuine. I'm grateful for his hands on my hips as I rise to greet him. Curving my shoulders against the top of the passenger compartment, I lean forward and hitch my tiny skirt higher, baring my shaved mound. We both groan as I lower myself onto him inch by shivering inch, my pussy molding to his rigid dick.

When I've got him, when I'm full, I reach behind me and work the hooks on my bra. As my breasts spill free, the money he gave me drifts to his belly. I pout a little, and he says, "Should have planned better than that."

"I was thinking about other things." To demonstrate, I slip my fingers into the back of my skirt. I've kept the handcuffs there, one dangling free outside the denim, the other pressing hard into my ass. "I believe this was part of your request?"

His cock moves before his lips do, twitching hard enough to make me plant a hand on his chest for balance. But then I hand him the key, trusting him to keep me safe. When he slips it into a cupholder in the driver-side door, I close the first cuff around my right wrist. I hold it up, showing him how tight I've set the bond.

Another hard jerk of his cock, but this time I'm expecting it so I don't lose my balance. Instead, I bring both hands behind my back. I close the second cuff around my left wrist. The angle of my joined hands raises my ribcage, pushing my bare breasts higher. I need to lean forward in the enclosed space to avoid the steering wheel.

"Oh sweet fuck," Trap says, rasping out each syllable like a prayer. But then I start to move, and all his words begin to run together.

With my hands pinned behind me, I need his strong hands on my hips to hold me steady. I rock forward on my knees, sliding up the glorious length of his cock. Before I lose him, though, I clench my inner muscles, making him grunt in surprise. By the time I ease back down, matching my aching pussy lips to the tight curls that frame his cock, he's digging into my waist hard enough to leave bruises.

This is what he's taught me—actions and words. I know his *cock* fills my *pussy*. My *snatch*. My *cunt*. I know I feel so full because he's stretching my *taint*. I know my *clit* is hot and hard, desperate for the moments when I lean all the way forward, when I grind against him hard enough to send arrows up my spine.

All the times we've fucked, I've never been on top. I've never had complete control of how fast we move, how slow, how deep he spears me.

But I've always been a quick student.

I find my perfect balance. I learn my ideal speed. I'm driving the massive power that's building between us, in charge, in control.

I break our rhythm because I know I can. I pause at the top of an arc, thighs quivering, pussy aching to be full again. I tease him. I bait him. I hover to show him I'm in charge.

And he twists beneath me. His cock slides free from my greedy slit. Holding me steady, he wriggles higher in his seat, shifting his body closer to the back of the vehicle.

I'm startled by the change in our positions, quivering at the loss of his dick inside me. Aching, empty, I wait for him to say I should suck his cock, which is now in range of my lips. He'll want me to drink every drop of his cum. I'll beg for more.

But that's not where he's pushing me. That's not what he needs.

His fingers roam from my hips to my tits. He pinches my nipples, hard enough to make my eyes water. And then he pulls me down, framing his cock with my breasts. He makes a channel and pumps it hard, slicking my tender skin with pussy juice and spit.

He calls me his princess. He calls me his queen. He squeezes me to the point of pain, past it, beyond. He's bucking faster now. Harder. He's lost his language, forgotten his words, all but one: *fuck, fuck, fuck.*

When he comes, he bellows a single wordless note, strung between pain and shattering release. He paints my tits, hitting my chin, my cheeks, my lips. He shudders and groans until he's drained.

When he finally frees me, I collapse across his belly. His cum slips from my chest, matting the line of dark hair that points to his sated cock. I'd run my fingers through it if I could, if my arms weren't still cuffed behind my back. I settle for licking my lips, for swallowing what I can reach.

He pulls me higher on his body, smearing his chest with the

mess on mine. He finds my mouth with his. His tongue sweeps against mine, hot and hard, and the banked fires inside me explode into new flame, burning away any thought of the ache in my shoulders, of the hard edge of the cuffs biting into my wrists.

His fingers slip between my thighs. He finds my vibrating clit. He strokes it, once, twice, three times, four.

Power gathers inside me like a storm cell thickening from clouds. He slips a finger inside me, but I'm too wet to squeeze it, too slick to hold him tight.

I need more. I need him. I need, I need, I need…

He points his fingers like a duck's beak, shaping all four fingers and his thumb into a long, narrow cone. I'm soaked as he pushes into me, stretching me, pulling me. He flexes his wrist to find the best approach. He catches my gaze, holding me, waiting for me, and when I'm truly ready, his whole hand sinks home.

I thought I was full when I rode him. I thought I was stretched by his magnificent cock. I thought all my nerves had fired, that I'd felt everything my body was designed to feel, that I knew every type of pleasure Travis Prince could give me.

But this is something I've never imagined. This is Trap holding me like I've never been held before.

His fingers shift inside me, curling into a fist. The heat and the hardness and the size of his hand… His knuckles press a secret place somewhere deep inside me, somewhere no one has ever touched before. And he forms a single word, fierce and proud and impossible to deny: "Come."

I fold.

I shatter.

I collapse around him and over him and somehow, impossibly, through him.

He waits until I stop sobbing before he eases his hand free. He kisses my damp eyelids as he retrieves the key from the cupholder. He supports my arms as he opens the cuffs, first the right and then, when I can bear it, the left. His arms fold over me. His ruined shirt tucks around me. He cradles me forever in the darkness of the car.

But I finally find the strength to move again. I push off his shoulders. I navigate the ridiculous console between our luxurious bucket seats. I collapse on the passenger side, realizing for the first time that I've lost both shoes; they must be somewhere near the gas and brake pedals.

Trap raises his seat. He strips off his shirt. He passes it to me with a rueful laugh. It takes all my meager energy to push my arms through his sleeves, to gather the pleated shirt close across my pearl-dusted breasts. He retrieves my bra from somewhere near his toes, along with a few damp hundred-dollar bills.

"Well," Trap says as he passes it all to me. "I think we'll both remember enough details to satisfy the cops."

We're still laughing when he pulls out of the alley and turns toward home.

18

TRAP

I look up from my phone as Alix enters the kitchen. "I just got an email," I say. "Three boxes of books have shipped from Oxford University Press."

"Great," she says.

I have to admit, I expected her to be a little more excited. It's only three fucking boxes, but it's the start of the best goddamn private art history collection in the United States.

But then it hits me. She's probably worried about space. About where she's going to put all those books.

"I've been thinking," I say. "We've got those three conference rooms on the ground floor of the office tower. With all the online meetings we have these days, we hardly ever use them. What if we have the architect draw up plans to convert two into a library?"

"Good idea."

Then why does she sound like I just suggested she design her own fucking tomb? I know the books mean a lot to her. I understand they're replacements for the originals, for the ones that burned in the fire at Herzog's house. But I want them to be more than that. I want them to be the core of the library she builds for herself.

I try again. "You'll need to store them until everything's arrived, or almost everything. Will it work, to keep them in your gallery in the warehouse?"

"Sure."

That's the first time I've mentioned the goddamn gallery since I had Leo dragged out and put in the hospital. We haven't talked about the table I had carted off to the junkyard. About the fucking cart I sent down to maintenance, along with all its tools.

I should have told her I was having the floor replaced before I did it. That I had the gallery painted. But I wanted to make it easy for her. I wanted to give her a chance to forget her whole fucked-up plan.

I wanted to make her happy. *Want* to make her happy. Now.

So I try one last thing. "You know you can hire someone to help, right? If you want to bring in a librarian, someone who can give you ideas about the best way to organize the books, maybe do the grunt work. We can make it a permanent position. The collection's going to grow."

"I'll think about it."

Maybe she's just tired.

I get her what she needs. A cup of fucking coffee.

When she reaches out to take it, I see the bruises on her wrists. They're angry and dark, with ugly little scabs tracing the places my handcuffs broke her skin.

I'm a fucking monster.

I made her wear the cuffs. I forced her to ride me—sweet Jesus how she rode me!—and then I fucked her incredible tits. I remember thinking as I pushed her boobs together, as I crushed them against my cock, that I could really get the grip I needed, that I could force the perfect angle because her arms were out of the way.

Shit. Are her tits as bruised as her wrists? Did I leave deep purple prints everywhere I squeezed?

"Princess…" I say, putting down the coffee carafe so I can take her hand. I bring the bruised line to my lips and brush it with the tip of my tongue. "Why didn't you say something?"

"I'm fine."

"You're not fine. I should have taken care of you." I know better. In the past, I've always *been* better. My only excuse—and I know it isn't valid—is that the whole scene blew my mind. The raunchy wrongness of fucking a whore in my car in the shadows of some dark alley…

I start to head upstairs. "Let me get the salve now."

"I'm fine," she says again. "They're just a few bruises."

Standing here in the kitchen, with sunshine streaming through the long line of windows, wearing jeans and a T-shirt, with a busy Sunday's tasks running through my mind, I feel like last night happened to a different man. I know Alix and I were simply going over facts, preparing for potential murder charges against us. But something else happened in that car.

We were different people.

We were the Trap and Alix we might have been if Klaus Fucking Herzog had never lived. If Alix's jizzstain brother had never fucked up her life.

It was a game. I know that. She isn't a whore. She's never been a whore.

But for those couple of hours, she wasn't Alix, either. She wasn't a woman who's been beaten, punished, who needed to fight for her life.

I liked that Alix.

I mean, I *love* the Alix that's real. I love the woman who's smart, who's brave, who's stronger than I'll ever be, no matter how many pounds I can bench press in the gym downstairs.

But I *like* the woman who was sly. Who flirted. Who worked

me over, upping my offer, taking me for what she needed. Hell, I like the woman who can take my fist. The woman who shatters into a million pieces around my entire wrist because I tell her to.

"I'm fine," she repeats, pulling her hand from mine.

I need to get to my office. I'm supposed to be planning the next Diamond Ring outing. There's still the delicate matter of handling the Ring members and their decisions about whether to pay the Herzogs' fucking blood money.

I want to take Alix to bed. I want to wrap her wrists in gauze and wait on her forever. I want to take her away from all this, fly her to the moon, or maybe just to Bora Bora.

But I settle for telling her, "I love you." I allow myself only a quick kiss on her lips. And I try to tell myself she means it when she says, "I love you too."

It doesn't matter that she refuses to meet my eyes.

That can't be important.

Fuck.

19

ALIX

I know Trap wanted more this morning. My short answers worried him. The bruises on my wrists freaked him out.

He didn't do anything wrong.

I was fine with the scene in the Hummer. After I got past the initial threat of frostbite, it was fun to wear fancy lingerie and sky-high shoes. Being on top turned me on more than I ever thought possible. I loved how he used my breasts, loved that they're so exciting to him.

I loved his hand inside me. His fist, even bigger than his cock. The feeling of his knuckles pressing against my inner walls.

I loved coming on command.

There wasn't a second in that car when I considered using my safeword. I knew he'd honor it if I did. I knew he'd keep me safe. But I didn't need it. Not while we were playing.

But when we got home… When I headed upstairs, clutching his wet and crumpled hundred-dollar bills…

I wish there was some way my safeword could erase that.

Trap bought me. And not just in the game we played at the train station.

I get it. He's a billionaire. He's got enough money to last a dozen lifetimes.

But I don't have anything. If not for his generosity, I wouldn't have the phone in my pocket. The clothes on my back. I'd be out on the street, without a job, a home, a car… I owe him everything.

And in some terrible, twisted way, that makes him the same as Herzog.

That's not fair. Trap has never hurt me in a way I didn't long for. I'm not a prisoner here. I could leave this absolute second.

Trap is not Klaus Herzog. But he's sort of, kind of, in ways I can't really explain to myself… He's like one of Herzog's special guests. I'm the girl with the willing mouth and the ready cunt to meet his every fantasy.

That's not fair either. He meets my fantasies too. He takes control. He gives me orders. He tests me and he stretches me and he makes me do things I never dreamed I could do.

Every time we're together, I can pretend I'm just his good girl. I'm not sick. I'm not twisted. I'm not so turned on by the thought of all the ways he hurts me that I'm starting to pant right here in the kitchen.

But if that's the case—if I really *do* want to be hurt—then what was the problem in Herzog's house?

I can *say* the special guests abused me. I can *say* that I was raped. But did those visitors ever know I wasn't there with full consent? Isn't it possible—just maybe—they thought we were playing a game? The same game Trap and I play?

It's different. I know that.

Trap gives me a safeword. He showers me with gifts. He says he loves me, and I know I love him.

But did I really let the special guests know I wasn't willing? Did I fight back? Did I do my best to protect myself?

Herzog kept the tapes. He must have thought they'd be worth millions.

What if he was wrong? What if the videos only show that I was weak? That I was stupid? That I deserved every single thing that happened to me?

I need to check. Need to see the truth. But it seems wrong to watch the videos inside Trap's house. They're filthy. Perverted.

So I collect a woolen blanket. I take my stuffed panda, because I need something to hold onto, an anchor, a friend. I pick up my computer, and I head outside to the chaise lounge, to see if I've misunderstood the videos all along.

20

TRAP

The best thing about being a billionaire is that I make the fucking rules.

I don't want to spend the day planning a party for a bunch of goddamn clients to bitch about the blackmailer trying to put all our asses in a sling? Fuck it.

I get to leave my office, cross my parking lot, enter my house, and screw the living daylights out of the woman I love.

Which would be a hell of a lot easier to do if she was upstairs in our bedroom. Or in the guest room she's appropriated for its closets. Or in the kitchen, the dining room, or on the back patio.

Alix has disappeared into thin air.

For just a moment, my heart stops. I remember how it felt to watch her running down my driveway, fleeing in the middle of the night. I remember the blow to my chest when she escaped to the Dover Lodge, preferring a lumpy mattress and a leaky shower to spending another second with me. I remember being gutted when I drove away from Klaus Herzog's haunted mansion, knowing my princess wasn't herself, certain she wasn't safe, but not able to do a fucking thing to make her understand.

An ice-cold vise tightens around my balls. But that's when I hear it—a jumble of voices, muted like the waa-waa-waa of grown-ups in *A Charlie Brown Christmas.*

The noise is coming from the basement, from the Olympics-quality gym I've got installed down there.

I open the door near the kitchen and head down the stairs.

The sound system is off. The lights are off. The treadmill, the elliptical, the Peloton bike—they're all still. No one's on the Pilates reformers or the TRX. The free weights are untouched.

The only equipment being used is a simple bench.

Alix straddles it, her back to me, her knees bent forward so her toes just touch the ground. For a heartbeat, I feel her sitting on top of me like that, grinding against my cock, driving us both toward an explosion.

But she's not fucking the bench. Her arms fold around her belly like she's trying to keep from puking. A blanket has slipped off her shoulders; it's slumped on top of a black and white lump that I finally realize is the fucking stuffed animal I won for her at the fair.

She's staring at a computer screen. It's the only light in the room, but it's magnified by the wall of mirrors behind the free weights, echoed and repeated until the entire gym is bathed in silver light.

Alix is watching a black-and-white movie. I already know the set. I know one of the actors. I'm certain about the plot. And the rage that detonates inside my skull almost leaves me blind.

Almost.

But not quite.

Because I can still see Alix on the screen, tied spread-eagle to a metal frame. Her chin has sunk to her chest. She's naked, except for a length of iron chain around her waist. She's got clips, too. A pair of them are screwed onto her nipples, tight enough to turn the tips black. Another is buried between her legs. The camera angle's shit, but I'm sure it's fastened to her clit. A weight hangs from it, swinging between her knees.

A man stands in front of her, facing away from the camera. His back is covered with hair, like a gorilla. Even his ass is hairy. He's clutching a riding crop in one hand and he's jerking off with the other. He calls to someone out of the frame. "I thought you said this one had spirit?"

A disembodied voice sounds amused. It's Klaus Herzog. I could testify to his voice in a court of law. He says, "She does. You just have to give her the right motivation. Piss on her."

"What?"

"Take your cock and piss on the lazy bitch."

The gorilla guy doesn't know what to do with the crop. He starts to put it on the ground. Changes his mind. Tucks it beneath his arm and repositions it twice when it starts to slip.

Finally, he's figured out the mechanics most of us learned in kindergarten. He grabs his cock and pisses, doing his best to paint her from tits to twat.

The sound system is good enough to catch the splatter of liquid on plastic. There's a drop-cloth under the metal frame, which means this horror show can only get worse.

Alix on the screen moans. She does her best to rally. Raises her chin. Opens her eyes. Stares at both men without saying a word.

Herzog's voice again: "Some horses won't run if you don't give them the whip."

The hairy cumwipe swats Alix with the crop, his wrist bent, no follow-through. He goes for her flank, like she really is some sort of animal. She flinches, but she doesn't make a sound.

Offscreen, Herzog says, "You need to show her who's master."

Another pansy-ass flick.

"No," Herzog says. "Turn this way. Use your whole arm. Put your weight behind it. Let her know who's really boss."

The shitbird grips the crop like it's a live rattlesnake. His arms juts out, stiff as a board. He turns to the side like he's sizing up a tee shot, and he pulls his arm back to get full momentum.

I could stare at the asshole's hard-on, the dick he's pumping even as he adjusts his stance. I could focus on the liquid poison of Herzog's voice, coaching him to smack her clit, to follow through by dragging down the weight between her knees. I could study the look of terror on onscreen Alix's face, the way she tries to shift her bound legs, how she tries to escape the blow she knows will come.

But I barely notice any of that, because I know this motherfucking son-of-a-bitch's face.

"What the actual fuck?" I bellow.

Alix jumps like I've electrified the gym bench.

Onscreen, she screams, a ragged wail that rips open something deep inside me. Before I can think, I shoulder past her in real life, stumbling over the blanket and the goddamn stuffed bear. I slam the computer shut and heave it to the floor, hoping to hell I'm breaking the screen. As the gym plunges into darkness, I demand, "What the fuck are you doing?"

"It was too cold outside," she says, like that's a perfectly reasonable response. "I didn't want to watch this in the house. So I came down here."

I can't see her face. I can only read her tone. And she might as well be telling me she felt like watching a re-run of *I Love Lucy*.

"I don't care about the goddamn weather. When the fuck did Bart Carver come to Herzog's house?"

"Who?"

I can stumble to the wall, find the light switch, make it right. But then I'll have to look her in the eye. I'll have to see her face, and she'll see mine.

I keep us in the dark. "Carver," I say. "Bartholomew P. Carver."

"That name sounds familiar..." She trails off, like she's trying to remember. The asshole pissed on her, beat her, and I'm willing to bet did a hell of a lot more twisted shit, but she's acting like she can't remember the name of a guy who signed her yearbook.

"The fuckwad on the screen," I say.

"Herzog called him Counselor."

Counselor.

I've sat across the table from the asshole in monthly Chamber of Commerce meetings for the past two years. I've greased his palm the way I've gotten to everyone who can help the freeport stay in business. I pretended like he was a fucking genius, like his dumbshit *Be Aware in Delaware* campaign would bring a shitload of business to our fine state.

Counselor. Bartholomew P. Carver *is* a lawyer. He's also Delaware's chief law enforcement officer. The head of the state's Department of Justice.

He's the Attorney General of Delaware.

And he just turned into a "get out of jail free" card for Alix and me.

21

ALIX

I thought I'd feel like a little girl playing dress-up, with my black sheath dress and my sensible pumps. I've covered the bruises on my wrists with careful makeup. I'm wearing a pearl choker and matching earrings. I'm carrying an actual briefcase.

I look like a corporate executive, or an investment banker, or a lawyer. Which might be why Bart Carver's assistant doesn't recognize me until she hears my name.

"Travis Prince and Alix Key to see Mr. Carver," Trap says.

The assistant's eyes go wide. She's clearly seen the Herzog video. She's picturing me in my Marilyn Monroe costume, stabbing a man to death while Trap looks on.

She has to swallow twice before she manages a professional smile and an aggressive tone. "Do you have an appointment?"

She won't meet my eyes. But she glances toward a container on her desk, taking a quick inventory of all the pointy things in the vicinity—a letter opener, a pair of scissors, a battery of ballpoint pens. I wonder what she'd do if I lunged for one of them.

"If we had an appointment," Trap says reasonably, "you'd have it on your computer."

The woman's heavily glossed lips purse in annoyance. "Mr. Carver is a very busy man. I'd be happy to schedule an appointment for you for some date in the future." She taps her keyboard and glares at her screen. "He's got an opening Thursday after next, October 22. At three thirty."

"Sorry," Trap says without glancing at the calendar on his phone. "That doesn't work for me."

She expresses her frustration with a short sigh. "The next appointment after that is the following Wednesday. Ten a.m."

"Yeah," Trap says, "That's no good either. I'd like to see him today."

She flattens her hands on her desk, and I wonder if she's tempted to strangle him. All this time, she's avoided looking at me. She takes a deep breath, like she's demonstrating the concept of *patience* for a couple of four-year-olds. When she speaks, she molds each word with exaggerated clarity. "Mr. Carver is busy today. He can't see you. You need to choose another time."

Trap turns to me and gestures toward two nearby chairs. "Shall we make ourselves comfortable?" he asks.

"That won't change my mind or Mr. Carver's schedule," the woman says tartly.

"We'll see about that," Trap says.

I take a seat and pick up today's *News Journal.* Offering the sports page to Trap, I dive into the Lifestyle section. I can't say that I'm really interested in the latest advice columns or the most recent Hollywood scandal. There's a review of a new restaurant in downtown Wilmington, and their salads sound interesting. Maybe we can head there for dinner, after we finish with Bart Carver.

Trap makes a big deal out of trading newspaper sections with me, shaking out the pages with a maximum amount of noise. The assistant ignores him.

That's the same way she ignores our reading the front-page section and the local news. The way she ignores our helping ourselves to coffee from the single-serve machine in the corner. The way she ignores my request for the key to the women's restroom and, later, Trap's demand for the men's.

I study the Delaware flag in the corner, wondering who decided it was a good idea to include two men, three farm crops, a ship, and a date on one single banner. I count the books on the shelves to my right, curious about the last time a lawyer actually looked up anything on paper, because I assume all of that is online. I flex my wrists, trying to decide if the makeup hides my bruises or makes them more obvious. That session in the Hummer really did a number on them.

Trap is edgier than I am, even though we've planned this excursion for a week. He checks his phone every few minutes. He gets up and paces. More than once, he stands beside the assistant's desk, looming like a thunderstorm until her icy glare sends him back to his seat.

During the three and a half hours that we sit there, the assistant goes into Carver's office six times. The last time, I look at the briefcase sitting by my feet. "Maybe if we let him know what we have," I start to say.

But Trap shakes his head. "Not going to tip my hand."

Technically speaking, it's *my* hand. So when the assistant comes out and resumes her space at her desk—hands on keyboard, feet tucked primly beneath her—I get up and stand directly in front of her.

"Does Mr. Carver know we're waiting?"

Her gaze slips sideways, toward her computer screen. Her jaw is carved out of stone. She might as well order up a billboard: She hasn't said a word to her boss.

"Look," I say, planting my hand on her desk. She glares at me with outright hatred, but I don't give her a chance to speak. "You seem to be very good at your job. But if Mr. Prince and I walk out of here today without seeing Mr. Carver and he finds out that he had a chance to avoid… Well, it won't be fair for the blame to fall on you. But I promise. It will."

She doesn't want to help me. But even more than that, she doesn't want to pull together her resumé for another job.

She rolls her eyes and flings herself out of her chair like she's a put-upon teen. But she disappears through the double doors for the seventh time.

"What was that?" Trap asks when we're alone. "Some sort of mind control?"

I shake my head. "Simple psychology. I made eye contact. Spoke fast. Used some charismatic terms. And I leveraged her fear of her boss."

"Remind me not to negotiate with you."

"You have other ways of getting what you want."

The instant heat in his eyes tightens something deep inside me. After our session in the car, I was afraid I would never feel this way again. Fighting a pang so sharp I can barely take a full breath, I say, "Stop it."

"Stop what?" He pretends to be innocent.

"Not here." I didn't think it was possible to hiss two words without an S, but I manage.

"Why not?" he asks, like it's reasonable to even consider making out—or more—right here. "Wait! Are you going to use your psychology magic tricks on me? We've got the eye contact thing down."

We do. I should look away. I could pretend to fiddle with my briefcase. I could study the titles on those legal books again. I could close my eyes and count to ten—anything to break the bond between us.

But now that it's back, I don't want to break that bond. Not this second. Not here. Not ever.

"Mr. Prince?" The assistant is back in the doorway. "Ms. Key? Mr. Carver will see you now."

"Thank you," I say, because it's another psychological trick to reward someone when they've done what you want. I'm pretty sure Trap isn't feeling as generous.

As we move toward the doors, I feel his hand on the small of my back. It's a little more pressure than necessary. A little more contact than I need, strictly speaking.

But I know what he's saying. He's offering support. And I don't know how much I need it until we're actually standing in Bart Carver's office.

He's shorter than I remember. Fatter. A slick of sweat shines on his upper lip.

"Bart," Trap says, not bothering to shake hands. "Glad you could make time to see us."

"What the hell do you think you're doing, coming to my office like this?"

"I didn't think you'd want to discuss this at our next Chamber of Commerce meeting," Trap says. "By the way, you remember Alix Key, don't you?"

He bristles. "Of course I do. I remember every alleged murderer currently being investigated by Delaware police. Every alleged accessory after the fact, too."

Trap shakes his head, like he's just heard a very sad story. "That's not the way you want to play this, Bart."

"You think I'm playing? In case you've forgotten, I'm the Attorney General for the state of Delaware. The two of you are represented by counsel. It's the height of impropriety for you to be here without your lawyers."

"I don't know, Bart. I'd say the height of impropriety is raping a woman. Along with assault and battery. Are those the right charges? For pissing on someone and beating the crap out of her with a riding crop? I'm not a lawyer, but there has to be something on the books for torture, right?"

There's a long moment when everything stops. I can't feel my heartbeat. My lungs don't expand for breath. I'm waiting, waiting, waiting, and Trap is curling his fingers like he's about to take a swing, now that the ugly words are out of his mouth.

Bart Carver stands frozen like a rabbit when a hawk soars overhead. Call it my psychological training, call it the survival instinct of a woman kept as a slave for three years, call it nothing more than women's intuition, but I can read every one of his thoughts as if they're written on his face in ink.

He's stunned that Trap knows the truth.

He's astonished that I told anyone; he must have thought I was too out of it at the time to remember—or maybe too ashamed to speak.

He's frightened that he's alone with two people who are already suspected of murdering a man connected with his crimes.

But ultimately, he's confident that it's my word against his. He's a respected government official, and I'm a deranged nut case whose video has been watched more than twelve million times.

"Get the fuck out of my office," he says. "Before I call security."

"Wrong answer," Trap says.

Carver goes for his phone. At the same time, I slam my briefcase down on his desk. I thumb the locks, and they sound like gunshots. I reach inside and take out my laptop computer.

Trap and I talked about this. We considered bringing a thumb drive. We thought about putting the video on a website and giving Carver the address. We thought about printing stills and letting him wonder what else we have in our possession.

But ultimately, we want to make him go away. Him and his prosecutors and the threat of a criminal case that will destroy our lives. Our lives, and the life of Braiden Kelly, because his face has been exposed too.

We can't leave Carver with any doubt at all, with any hope of escape.

So I open the computer. I press the gray triangle in the middle of the screen. I turn the device toward him, and I watch him realize his professional life is about to end.

The video plays without sound. That's the way Herzog planned things—he kept himself out of the frame to make it seem like Carver acted entirely on his own.

I don't watch the screen. I'll never forget a frame of what happened.

I don't watch Trap either. I can still see his face reflected in the basement gym's mirrors. I can see his rage and disgust and pain as my body is abused.

I watch Carver.

I watch denial: That's not him. That's not me. That's not something that actually happened.

I watch rage: Herzog had no right to film him. Trap and I can't possibly have this proof.

I watch bargaining: He has a reason for what he did, a justification. He'll tell us if we let him.

I watch depression: He can't cope. He can't go on. He'll never survive.

I watch acceptance.

All the stages of grief, like a movie sped up to triple speed. Carver bounces through them so fast I'm a little surprised he's still standing.

"Okay," he says. "I'll announce my retirement next week. I'll call a press conference next Friday."

"Forget it, motherfucker," Trap says. "You'll do it tomorrow."

"That imposs—"

"Tomorrow, asshole. Or I cut off your dick, put it in a blender, and feed it to you through a goddamn straw."

"No," I say, and I think it's possible that both men had forgotten I'm here. I turn to Carver. "You *will* call a press conference for tomorrow. But you're going to use it to make the cases against Trap, me, and Braiden Kelly disappear. The cops have no evidence. The murder video is a deep fake. Case closed."

Trap gives a tight little nod. He trusts me, even if I'm stepping on all his plans. That gives me the confidence to go on.

"And if any cases come up in the future," I say. "Against us, or against Diamond Freeport, or against any of our clients, you'll make them go away. Your office has nothing to do with Klaus Herzog or his brothers, Jonas and Ansel. You have no interest in their AI-nonsense videos."

"I can't promise—"

"You can," I assure him. It feels like I'm swinging a sledgehammer. I have all the power in the world, but my bones might shatter from the weight. "If you don't want me going public."

He splutters. He starts half a dozen sentences, every one an argument about how he can't protect me, can't protect Trap, can't protect the Diamond Ring.

But his eyes fall on my computer screen. On the devastating freeze-frame of him standing on a sheet of plastic, looming over my torn and bleeding body. The empty metal frame towers above us like a gallows, sealing his fate.

"But that's not all," I say to Carver. I'm shoving down my instinct to back off. Hardening my heart to do what I have to, to keep us safe—me, Trap, Braiden, and the rest. "No matter what, you will *not* resign. You're staying in office until your term ends three years from now. And you're running again and again and again—until the voters in this state finally have the sense to put a decent man in office."

It takes a moment for the penny to drop. But when it does, he looks at me with horror.

"That's right, Counselor," I say. And it *is* horrible—my power over him. I never would have had it if he hadn't attacked me first. But he did. And I do. And the strength I feel scorches something deep inside me. "You're staying in office," I say. "And just to celebrate, Trap and I will send you a little present—a private, untraceable phone. Make sure you answer it, any hour of the day or night. Because this video goes public the first time you fail to do exactly what we want."

He puffs like a bantam rooster. “I can’t—”

Trap’s fist slams down on the desk with a fury that startles even me. Carver turns whiter than his office walls.

“You can,” I assure him, meeting his terrified eyes. “And you will. Trust me. It’s truly amazing, the things a person can do to survive.”

Trap picks up the computer. I retrieve my briefcase. And both of us leave the office, not bothering to look back on the ruined man we leave behind.

22

TRAP

"Holy shit," I say, the instant the elevator doors close behind us. "You don't fuck around."

Alix hunches her shoulders, all that glorious power and strength evaporated. "I'm sorry I stepped on your plan," she says.

"Step on anything you want. You were fucking amazing."

She's as pale as a legal summons when the elevator opens onto the parking garage. We walk to the Range Rover, side by side.

When I open the passenger-side door, I lean close and whisper in her ear, "Any chance you're free for a date? I just got good news, and I'm willing to pay for more than just the girlfriend experience."

I thought she'd laugh. Maybe jack up the price and take me for a couple thou. I didn't think she could top her black-bra-and-mini-skirt combo, but the lady-lawyer look is definitely growing on me.

But she brushes a kiss against my cheek and says, "Honestly? I'm starving. There's supposed to be a new restaurant over on Union Street. Can we go there?"

"Of course."

I'm such an asshole. We spent hours waiting for Little Miss Tight-ass to let us through the door. It's no surprise Alix wants to eat.

We make our way to Union Street. The place has valet parking, which is good, because I'm suddenly starving too, and the thought of looking for parking is enough to make me growl. I hand over the keys, and we head inside the restaurant.

No one recognizes us. Maybe that's because the video's been out for weeks. Maybe we're old news, and people are more interested in real housewives or the latest Hollywood scandal or some politician who can't keep his dick in his pants. Maybe it's because Alix and I are dressed like big-firm lawyers. I don't know why we aren't noticed, and I don't care.

We eat a normal dinner in a normal restaurant like normal people. I have to remind the waiter I wanted Dewar's, not Grey Goose, but he gets it right the second time. Alix's salad dressing isn't served on the side. My rare steak is closer to medium, but who really gives a fuck?

It takes almost two hours to work through appetizers, entrées, and desserts, and for once I'm not thinking about torture-porn videos, or billionaire tax schemes, or anyone anywhere named Herzog.

We talk about whether the guy outside, the one walking his dog, is wearing a toupée or if he's got the worst haircut in the world. We tell each other our dream meals—I never knew she had a thing for white chocolate bread pudding. We debate the funniest movie of all time, and how it's actually impossible that she's never watched *Monty Python and the Holy Grail*.

So it's a complete surprise when my phone rings as I'm tipping the valet. It's Throck. "Just a second," I tell him, as I gun the engine and turn down a side street. I block a fire hydrant and put the car in Park.

"Okay," I say. "You're on speaker. Alix is with me."

If he's concerned about attorney-client privilege this time, he doesn't make a complaint. Instead, he says, "I have very good news."

"We're listening," I say.

I don't realize I've taken Alix's hand until Throck wraps things up, hundreds of pauses and fifteen minutes later. "What guarantee do we have that the prosecutors won't change their minds?" I ask.

"Well, technically…double jeopardy hasn't…attached because no claim has been made."

"How long do they have to come after us?"

"There's no statute of limitation on murder… And we have to assume…that's what the charge would be."

"So we live with this hanging over our heads forever?"

"Technically…well…yes… Although I have to say…. With Ms. Rodriguez off the case…. The prosecutor who phoned me…couldn't make any promises…but he seemed to think the office…has lost all interest in this case…. Higher-ups don't want the risk…. It's too high profile…. So much confusing technology…no jury will ever understand…."

It's the longest statement Throck has ever made. But it's worth paying for, just to know Alix and I are clear for the foreseeable future.

Throck has more. Carver's making a formal announcement tomorrow morning. Alix and I should be available for a press conference tomorrow afternoon. We do that, and the fucking paparazzi should finally look for fresh blood somewhere else.

I end the call and sit back in my seat. Until this moment, I didn't realize how much the case was hanging over me. I can only imagine Alix felt it even more. I was only on the hook as an accessory. She was always the main target.

Once the phone is dark, I raise our joined hands. My lips

brush across her knuckles. I catch a whiff of something that smells like baby powder, and I realize it's the makeup she used to hide the bruises on her wrists.

"Hey," I say. "You were incredible today."

Her smile is exhausted.

I tighten my grip on her fingers. "It still pisses me off, though, that Carver won't pay for what he did."

She twitches one shoulder. "He'll face pressure for letting us off the hook. And who knows what the freeport will need before his term is up?"

With my free hand, I brush a curl from her cheek. "He may have political fallout. But that's nothing compared to what you've dealt with."

There's that tiny smile again. "We can't change the past."

She's right. I know she is. But I have to say, "You know if there was any way I could go back in time… If I could redo that night… If I could keep you tied to my bed instead of—"

"You and your ties," she says, but the joke sounds faint.

"I would have kept you safe. Herzog would have taken someone else…"

"Don't say that."

"Why the fuck not?" I'm angry—not with her, but with the madman who stole her from me.

"Because I survived. Someone else might not have walked out of that house." She pauses for a moment, and then she says, "And who knows where I'd be today, if I hadn't been there?"

"You'd be with me."

"Maybe. Probably. But—"

"*You'd be with me.*" I need her to say it. I need her to know it as thoroughly, as completely as I do.

"You're right," she says. "I'd be with you, no matter what."

She's saying the words I want to hear, exactly what I asked for. That should be right. That should be enough.

But it isn't, and I don't know how to ask for what I need.

She flexes her fingers between mine. "Okay?" And then, "It's been a crazy long day. Can we go home now?"

"Of course." I start the car and pull out into the street. It only takes an hour and a half to get home. But by the time I park the Range Rover in the garage, I realize the truth I've been trying to avoid for at least the past week.

I'm losing her.

And I don't know what to do.

23

ALIX

I couldn't tell Trap last night. He wouldn't understand.

When he helped me into the car, when he joked about our little train station game, that's all it was to him—something to laugh about. Something to get turned on by, just like he gets excited by ropes and gags and floggers.

But for me, it was something different. It was embarrassing. Degrading.

It shouldn't be. Trap and I play roles. That's what brought us together in the first place—our mutual need for secret, kinky sex.

I trust him in the bedroom. I know he'll never force me to do anything I don't want to do with my body.

But with my mind?

I'm not as sure.

And thinking about that as we sat in the car, as we ate our dinner, as we made the long drive back to the freeport… it made me sad. Sad and scared—because I don't know where this relationship is going. What happens if I can't play Trap's games? What happens if I just don't want to?

And there was something else that worried me last night. When Throck called, when we got the best news we could possibly hope to get, I wanted to share it with someone else.

I wanted to share it with Leo.

My entire life, I shared good news with my brother. Good grades—Mom and Dad took us out for ice cream. Given a solo in the eighth-grade choir concert—Leo celebrated with me in the school hallway. Getting into Sherman—Leo bought me a blue-and-green sweatshirt.

It's messed up, I know. Two weeks ago, I wanted to torture him, to kill him.

But now I feel like we've got a second chance. Or maybe a ninth chance, since he's been to rehab eight times before?

I know how that sounds. Every time I've said something like this in the past, I've lost someone—my family, my friends, my former fiancé. Now I'm terrified my brother will cost me Trap.

But things are different now. *I'm* different now. And after the past three years of hell, Leo must have changed too. That's the only way all of this makes sense.

I'm desperate for Trap to agree. I want him to say yes to the plan that kept me up all night. But first things first: I have to get past Susan Richards.

"Alix!" she says as I approach her office, across from Trap's.

"Good morning!" My voice is too loud. Too bright. I sound like an advertisement for coffee.

"I heard the good news on the radio as I was driving in this morning. I'm so glad the prosecutor has finally seen reason. You and Trap don't need that horrible fake video hanging over your heads any longer."

"I always knew the case *should* go away," I say with a confidence that's a lie. *I'm* the reason the case disappeared. Because I blackmailed a man. Because I used my power as a weapon. But I force a smile. "We're lucky it all came together."

Susan glances at the telephone console on her desk. "Trap just got off the phone," she says. "If you hurry, you can catch him before his ten o'clock."

I smile my thanks and duck into Trap's office, making sure the door is closed behind me. Susan might think I'm here to steal a quickie, but I don't care. I need the privacy because Trap and I are going to talk about Leo.

"Good morning," I say, crossing the office. I kiss his cheek before he can rise out of his chair. "I missed you when I woke up."

"I had a conference call with Deutsche Bank," he says. "Fucking time zones."

I sit down in the chair opposite his desk, but it's hard to find the right place for my hands. When I put them on the arms of the chair, I feel like I'm making some sort of demand. When I put them in my lap, I feel like a little girl.

I shift my feet and cross my ankles. That feels strange, so I try crossing my legs at my knees. My palms are sweating. I wipe them on my thighs.

The sun is reflecting off the bay in the distance. Work on the freeport's racetrack is going well; the grandstand is nearly complete. The solar panels on top of the house look like ocean waves breaking against the building's white stone.

"Just say it." Trap's voice is tight and low. He's gripping the arms of his chair, his fingers curled into claws.

I swallow hard. And then I do the bravest thing I've ever done with him—braver than going to his home that first night, braver than taking any of the toys in his bedroom, braver than facing down Bartholomew Carver.

I meet his eyes, and I say, "I want Leo to come and live at the freeport after he's discharged from the hospital."

"Oh, sweet Christ," Trap mutters. Something comes unpinned in his shoulders, and his entire body sags in something that looks an awful lot like relief.

"What did you think I was going to say?" I ask.

"Nothing," he says too quickly. "I didn't have any idea."

He's lying. He expected me to ask for something more. But I'm not about to push for details, not when he hasn't yet responded to my actual request.

Instead, I present the arguments I put together in the shower this morning. Point one: "He's been out of the real world for almost three years, and he needs some time to readjust." And two: "Jonas and Ansel won't take the attack on their warehouse lying down. We owe it to Leo to keep him safe from them." And three, the real reason, the one I dearly, truly hope I can share with Trap and have him understand: "I miss him. He's my brother, my *twin*, and despite everything that's happened, I want to keep him in my life."

"Tell Susan to move him into Swallowtail Cottage."

Swallowtail. That's one of the four guest houses on the freeport property. The furthest from our house.

My immediate response is to ask for something closer. Strawberry Cottage is practically in our back yard. Goldenrod overlooks the bay. Holly is carved out of the woods. It's the most isolated, where a challenging guest is least likely to be noticed.

But then I realize what Trap has just given me. He's allowing Leo to move onto the property. He's not adding layers of requirements. He's not making me choose between my brother and the rest of the world.

"Thank you," I say, very close to tears.

"He'll need clothes," Trap says gruffly. "And other basics."

The same as I did, when I escaped Klaus Herzog's grasp. This nightmare just goes on and on and on.

But Trap doesn't seem upset. Instead, he adds, "Get him what he needs. And when he's ready for a job, we'll see what we can find for him here."

"I—" But I don't have any way to finish that. So I say again, "Thank you."

Before I can add anything else, the intercom whistles on

Trap's desk. Susan's steady voice says, "Your ten o'clock is on line one."

"We've got the press conference at two," I say, and Trap nods.

Outside, I say to Susan, "My brother will be released from Dover General soon. Trap says we can set him up in Swallowtail, while he gets back on his feet."

Susan's fingers fly over her keyboard. "Consider it done. The kitchen is stocked with necessities, but if he has any favorites, just let me know."

I thank her and head back to the house.

This can work. This can really work. Leo will have the support he needs. He can continue to see the psychiatrist and the nutritionist who've been treating him at the hospital. He'll be removed from the temptations of the outside world. And he won't have to check into rehab. Won't have to live in a new facility, the same as all the old facilities where he's failed before.

Most important of all—he'll be close to me.

I owe Trap more than I can ever repay.

It's easy to come up with ways to thank him. I can imagine a blindfold tight across my eyes. A gag pressing against my lips. I rub my wrists and tighten my thighs and brace for the sting of a flogger that never comes.

I want it, as much as I know Trap does. I'd be excited, even if Leo wasn't moving into Swallowtail Cottage.

There's nothing wrong with that, is there?

There's no reason I can't soothe the aching places in my soul. I can bargain for the things I desire, even if my choice was once taken from me by a madman. I can want pain from one man, want punishment from Trap when Herzog left me reeling.

That's what freedom feels like. That's what it means to heal.

I almost have myself convinced when Trap steals into the house for an unexpected lunch break. I test my conclusions, all my justifications, screaming myself hoarse when Trap lets me come.

We're late to the press conference, which ignites a storm of speculation among the most avid paparazzi. But I can already sense boredom in most of the camera-waving troops. The shouts for our attention are fewer and less vigorous.

Trap and I read our prepared statements, avoiding any opportunity to editorialize. We thank Throck for all of his hard work, and we express our gratitude that we had the resources to deal with this matter when so many hard-working Americans would have been crippled or worse my such a potential miscarriage of justice.

We leave before the vultures are satisfied. But for the first time in weeks, I believe we've finally turned a corner. Our lives will get back to normal.

Or they would, if Jonas and Ansel Herzog were as easily disposed of as Bartholomew P. Carver.

24

TRAP

~

Who the fuck thought it would be a good idea to have monthly Diamond Ring meetings?

Oh. I did.

I latched onto the idea the first time the suggestion crossed Alix's lips—before I'd ever kissed those lips. Before they'd ever closed around my cock.

She said it would build business. Make the freeport's biggest clients loyal to me on a personal basis. Turn us into an exclusive group.

Well, it's a pretty exclusive group—the guys who watched Alix knife Klaus Herzog. The poor assholes who were on the hook as accessories after the fact, same as me. The motherfuckers who are right now toasting Bartholomew Carver with my vintage champagne, drunk out of my crystal glasses, ten days after the fuckwad folded.

"So tell the truth," Cole Wolf says. "Who'd you have to pay off to make the charges go away?"

"I didn't pay a cent," I say.

"What have you got on the AG?" Connor Boyle asks. He knows how the game is played. Actually, more than one game—in addition to running New York City's Irish Mob, he's the president and CEO of the largest green energy company in the Northeast.

I'm sure Boyle's seen his share of videos. Used them more than once to make a point for his family. But there's no way in hell I'm telling him about the Carver video. No way I'm ever saying out loud what Herzog made Alix do.

"I just walked into the motherfucker's office and told him we'd settle things the old-fashioned way," I boast. "He unzipped his pants, I unzipped mine, and we both put our cocks on the table. I won by a good six inches."

I hitch at my belt as more than one asshole fake-coughs, "Bullshit."

"So if you're through drinking my champagne," I say to all of them, "you can each take a key off that pegboard and see what's waiting outside."

The answer is six million dollars worth of souped-up stock cars. At first, I thought it was a stupid choice—a dozen vehicles to entertain a bunch of over-grown boys for one fucking night.

But then, I realized the cars could stay in the garage here at the track. Let new freeport clients take them out for a spin. Maybe sponsor a charity race somewhere down the line.

The cars have identical engines—Ford V-8s capped at 5.9 liters. They've all got new tires, with a dozen extra sets in the pit for quick replacement. Same chassis, just like official NASCAR vehicles. The fuel tanks are filled with Green E15.

Each of my guys'll take home his own fire suit and helmet as a little souvenir. I hired pit crews from the Dover Speedway; paid them triple overtime to get them here for the night.

Everyone in the Ring is laying side bets before they make it out the door. The Speedway's safety coordinator proposed running only two cars at a time, but these guys don't take kindly to suggestions. We're racing in heats of four, top two stay on the track. My money's on Sawyer Best to win it all.

I'm leaning against the unfinished grandstand, sipping an ice-cold bottle of Berg, when Braiden Kelly comes to slouch beside me. He keeps his eyes on the track as he takes a slug from his own water.

"Imagine my surprise when my lawyer called to say the prosecutor lost all interest in my case," he says, like we're talking about the weather.

"A lot of that going around these days."

"I owe you one. And I don't forget my debts."

I nod. We're both good at bookkeeping.

"How's Herself handling the news?" he asks.

"Like she just found a winning lottery ticket."

"And her brother?"

Kelly doesn't give a shit about Leo. But he's asking about the aftermath of our little game on the Philly docks. I shrug.

"The boyo looked to be in pretty bad shape," Kelly says.

"He was discharged from the hospital on Wednesday."

Kelly raises his eyebrows. Three and a half weeks is a long hospital stay, even for a strung-out head case kept chained to a table for years. But if Kelly thinks that was overkill, he keeps that to himself. "Could be dangerous," he says. "Out on the streets. A man could find himself in the middle of a war."

"He's staying here for a while. In one of the freeport guest houses." But that's not as interesting as what Kelly just said. "It's a war out there? You've got guys on the front line?"

"Let's just say your Krauts didn't appreciate being relieved of their inventory."

"How long will it take you to turn over that shit?" I'm genuinely curious. I have no idea how Kelly's business works.

He turns his head to the side and spits, like he's trying to get rid of a bad taste. "We dumped most of it."

"Dumped? You've sold it already?"

He shakes his head. "Dumped. We took it ten miles offshore

and tossed it overboard. Crash is the reason good lads and lasses are dying in the streets. None of the Irish families will touch the stuff. Ask your man Boyle."

"I just assumed…" I assumed he raided the warehouse for the financial gain of the drugs inside.

"Don't you worry," he says with a lopsided grin. "I've still got plenty to confess to Father Cullen, come Sunday. And the twenty keys of coke in your boyo's back room made it all worthwhile."

"Yo! Kelly!" Cole Wolf hollers from the track. "You're up next!"

Kelly pushes off from the wall and heads over to the cars. Boyle took the green one, so he'll have to be satisfied with flame orange.

I watch a couple of rounds. The noise of the engines is ferocious. Each driver makes at least one pit stop, mostly for the hell of it, and the scream of hydraulic tools adds to the chaos.

Gage Rider craps out after one heat and comes to grab a bottle of water. "Christ, that's loud," he says.

"Half the fun, right?"

He unzips his fire suit. Susan had to have one made special order to fit his shoulders. For that matter, the harnesses inside the car are meant for mere mortals, not the type of giant who straps on skates and chases a puck for fun.

"Speaking of fun," he says, putting on a pretty good act of looking casual as he stares out at the track. I only know he's tense because I'm standing two feet away and can see the muscle working at his jaw. "We've got a big Halloween party planned at the club. Your name's on the guest list."

The club. That would be Kynk, up in Brooklyn. Gage runs the joint on the side of his billion-dollar real estate empire. No wonder he bailed on the National Hockey League after only six years.

"Jack Strong?" I ask. That's the name he gave me last time.

He shakes his head. "Security wrote you up after that shit with the Herzogs. I figured a clean slate was a good idea."

I'm still pissed with Rider for how he handled things, throwing me out when I was only defending Alix.

"I put you down as Seymour Limpdick," he says.

And I guess Rider's still pissed with me. I keep my voice mild. "That should work well with the ladies."

"I figure you won't be there to hook up."

If he's giving me a lecture about how to treat Alix, I don't need his fucking input. But I ask, "Do I need a costume for this?"

"Same rules as before. Masks required. Clothing optional."

"That worked so well the last time."

"Sorry, man," he says. "Rules are rules."

"You can take your fucking rules and shove them up your ass." I take care to scrub any heat from my tone, but this whole conversation is pissing me off. Alix was hurt in his club. He can argue all he wants that she didn't use her safeword, but his security guys should have stepped in. And he had no business throwing me out on my ass when I took care of things.

He shrugs, and it's like I'm standing next to an earthquake. "What'll it take to make us right?" he asks. "We can fight, if you want. I'll give you one free swing."

My krav maga against his years of fighting on the ice. I'd be lucky to get away with bruised knuckles. More likely, I'd be nursing a concussion worse than the ones that ended his career.

"I'll pass," I say.

Another one of those earth-shattering shrugs. And then he makes his peace offering. "Jonas and Ansel are both on the guest list. I'm comping them a party room—private bar, food and drink specials, some orange-and-black fetish shit to make up for the hassle last time."

My temper gets the better of me. "Their motherfucking *hassle*—"

He rolls right over me. "That way, you'll know exactly where they are, all night long. I'm giving them the room closest to the kitchen."

Closest to the service entrance. All I have to do is get them out the door, the same way I planned last time. Best's team will do the wetwork.

It's a solid offer. A fair effort at unfucking my last visit.

"Thanks," I say. And because civilized men shake when they've made agreements to take out cocksuckers like the Herzogs, I offer Rider my hand.

His grip is firm, but not aggressive. Even so, the Beast that lives inside my skull wakes up to growl its displeasure. I tell it to go fuck itself as I tap my index finger against my thigh, five quick flicks. If Rider notices, he doesn't say a word.

Instead, he grabs another water bottle and turns back to the track. He's three steps away when I ask his shoulders, "What did you really put down for me, on the guest list?"

"Kent Clark," he says, without turning around.

So I'm the opposite of a superhero. Well, fuck. I can live with that. "Works for me."

He waves a hand before heading over to the pit. I check, but he's using all his fingers. For now, I'll count that as a win.

The Beast's still prowling around, stirred up by Rider's grip and the knowledge I'll be glad-handing my way through the rest of the Diamond Ring before they head home at the end of the night. Once again, I tell it to fuck off, but that works as well as it usually does. I squeeze out a five-count with my fist and when that doesn't work, I beat the water bottle against the grandstand wall.

Screw it. Time to take out the big guns. I pick up the last key on the table and head over to the track. "Okay you motherfuckers," I say when the guys look my way. "Let me show you how it's done."

I don't give a fuck if I win or not. I'm just hoping that shifting through the gears knocks out the goddamn Beast. Turns out, making the turns requires its own laser focus. I'm halfway through my sixth lap when I realize the animal in my head is down for the count.

I leave Wolf and Dubois in the dust. Best and I cross the finish line at virtually the same time. I make a note to install a camera for close finishes. And then I lead the Ring over to the tent, where a full bar and enough food for an army puts a cap on the night.

25

ALIX

"I'm heading out," Trap says.

I jump like a jackrabbit, completely surprised by his presence. I came to my gallery right after breakfast, and I've long since lost track of time. I've spent the past two weeks doing my best not to think about where Trap's going tonight. It turned out, what I really needed for distraction was box after box of glossy-paged coffee-table art books.

"Sorry," Trap says. "Didn't mean to startle you."

"I started looking at that Van Gogh catalog, and that made me think about the new Cezanne books that arrived last week, but I got distracted by these Monet waterlilies…" I could study those paintings for hours.

Or I could study Trap.

He's dressed all in black—black suit, black shirt, black silk tie. He must have showered and shaved right before he came over to the warehouse; I can smell his rosemary shampoo. His hair is a little long, just the way I love it, and something aches so hard in my chest I have to blink.

"For you," he says, holding out a white plastic bag.

"What is it?"

"Something to keep you busy while I'm gone."

I peer inside like there might be something living in there. I'm surprised to see dozens of candy bars—orange and brown and silver wrappings, the full-size ones that would have made little-girl me go crazy on Halloween.

"Trick or treat," he says, in response to my laugh.

"What if I choose trick instead?"

A light flares in his eyes, exactly the way I knew it would.

I shouldn't tempt him. He needs to meet his driver in the parking lot. He needs to get up to Brooklyn, to Kynk. He needs to take care of Jonas and Ansel Herzog before they come up with some new way to ruin our lives.

We've talked about it, all the gritty details. He made me say out loud that I didn't mind his going back to the club. I know he'll wear a black silk Lone Ranger mask. He'll leave his tie and shirt and jacket in the Green Room while he keeps his pants on, with knock-out drugs in his pocket. He'll prowl through the crowd, ignoring propositions from women and men alike, until he finds his prey in the private room Gage Rider promised.

I trust Trap.

With my life, I trust him.

But there are a million things that can go wrong, from a crash on the freeway to the Herzogs fighting back. There's a very real chance Trap won't return to the freeport.

And there's no way I can go to the club with him. The thought of entering Kynk is enough to make my pulse rate double. All I have to do is close my eyes, and I can see Jonas and Ansel, I can hear their commands, I can feel their cane slicing across my bare breasts…

Even if I manage to master my terror, I can't be there. My

presence would just distract him. He'd have to worry about my safety, on top of seeking out the brothers.

But words tear from my throat before I can smother them. "Don't go."

"Alix..." Trap says, and my name sounds like shredded tire retreads scattered across a freeway.

"We took care of Carver. Jonas and Ansel can't hurt us now. Us or the Diamond Ring. You don't have to do this. You can just stay home." I feel even more desperate than I sound.

Trap shakes his head. "You don't let rabid dogs roam the streets, just because you have a lock on your door."

"But *you* don't have to be the one to hunt them down."

"I do," he says.

Because of you.

He doesn't say the words, but I hear them, loud and clear. He needs to destroy Jonas and Ansel Herzog because the brothers hurt me. Because they could still come after me. Because I'll never truly be free as long as they live.

I should put the table between Trap and me. I should take my bag of candy and go. I should lock myself in our bedroom until he comes home tomorrow morning, until he tells me that all went well, that Jonas and Ansel Herzog will never hurt another living soul.

But I don't.

I set aside my candy bars and reach for a far better treat.

The metal of his belt buckle is cool against my fingertips, but the leather feels warm and supple. Alive. I slide it from his waist slowly, never looking away from his captivating green-brown gaze.

His breath catches as I loop the belt around my neck, and he groans a little when I pull it tight enough to feel a bite.

"If you have to leave me—" I whisper.

"You know I do," he interrupts.

"Then give us both something to think about while you're

on the road." I offer him the length of leather, arching my neck so he can see the belt's grip.

He steps away.

A disbelieving sound blooms in my throat, but he meets it with a low, smirking laugh. Turning to the gallery door, he uses his foot to shift the boxes that block it open. The lock snicks closed with a finality that shoots through my belly like liquid fire.

"Or were you planning to put on a show for anyone who happens by this afternoon?" he asks.

"No," I say, my voice breathy as I keep the belt tight. "This is only for you."

The light flares in his eyes again. His kiss, when he comes to me, is urgent and salty and crude. His teeth strike mine. His tongue pushes hard for mastery, and his fingers clutch at my hair. He pulls, hard, which makes me press my entire body closer to his.

The belt loosens around my neck as I reach for the buttons on his shirt. Still savaging my mouth, he lets go of my hair to shove my hands away. I go for his pants instead, fighting for the button, for the zipper, for the access I desperately need.

He pushes my fingers away again, and when I whine a protest, he laughs against my lips. "Eager little princess, aren't you?"

I try one more time. I reach inside his pants, sliding my hand toward the heat of his cock. Of course, he catches me easily, pulling me free before I can touch him. He catches both my wrists in one hand, using his other to strip his necktie free.

It only takes a moment for him to bind my hands—short, sharp motions that make me gasp. He's efficient with his knots; I can barely wiggle my fingers.

"Please," I beg, but he only shoves me toward the table. His grip on the back of my neck makes my knees go liquid, and he laughs as I steady my palms between the books.

"You made that much more difficult than it needed to be,"

he growls, and his complaint scrapes something raw and needy inside me. "And what does that mean?"

I'm so excited I barely manage to whisper, "I need to be punished."

"Exactly." Without warning, he yanks my yoga pants to my knees, taking my plain cotton panties with them.

I yelp in surprise, but he's already pressing his leg between my thighs. My fingers curl inside their silk bonds as he forces my feet wide, wider, until my panties are stretched between my knees.

He smooths his palm over my bare bottom, and I bite my lip to keep from moaning. His belt has slipped loose around my throat, making it easy for him to take it from me, to wrap the leather around his fist.

He traces my spine with the tip of the belt, knob by bony knob, and my thighs begin to tremble. I can't resist rising up on my toes, can't keep from rocking back, from pushing against his hand.

"Who's in charge here, Princess?" he asks.

"You are," I answer immediately.

"Your lips say one thing, but your ass says something else."

"You're in charge," I say stubbornly.

The flat of his hand falls on my bottom, just hard enough to sting. "So this ass is mine? I can do anything I want with it?"

"Yes," I say, and I try not to push against him, try not to lead. I fail.

Without warning, he shoves two fingers deep inside me. "And this soaking wet pussy? It's mine?"

"Yes." I vow not to twist on his hand, not to bring him deeper into my heat. I fail again.

He pulls out and finds my clit, pinching between his finger and his thumb. "And this clit? It belongs to me too?"

"Yes," I gasp, but the admission is almost lost as I swear I won't tighten my thighs around his wrist, in hopes he'll pinch again. One more time, I fail.

"I don't think you understand the concept of ownership, Princess."

"Then teach me," I gasp, because he knows my body. He knows what I need. He knows how to wind me tight, and how to release me, and I'll do anything to keep him here for even one minute longer.

Somehow, I'm surprised when the leather smacks my ass. The strike sends crimson lightning up my spine, and I picture the stripes he's just made, parallel lines left by either side of the belt.

Again, I want to beg. But Trap's in charge. He owns me. He decides what I deserve and what I don't deserve. He chooses exactly what to give me.

So my fists turn to marble and the cords in my throat become steel, but I don't say it. I don't move.

And he rewards me with another slash of the belt.

I need this. The stripes from the leather close a circuit in my skull, feeding pure bliss directly into my brain.

A third time, he strikes me.

A fourth, the hardest blow he's ever measured out for me.

Fifth, and my legs can't hold me anymore.

Sixth, and my belly presses against the table, my bound arms stretch in front of me, every muscle in my body goes rigid from the force of his belt against my desperate flesh.

I can't breathe, can't see, can't think. All my words have melted. I'm reduced to the pure fire Trap is painting on my body, the perfect pain he's etching on my soul.

I'm waiting for the blow that will destroy me. I'm spun and stretched and suspended in the absolute nowhere of the space between my cells. I'm nothing and everything. I'm past and present. I'm…

He drives into me from behind, his cock taking full possession of the pussy he staked a claim to, longer, harder, wider than his fingers. He pins me and he penetrates me, possesses every inch of me.

He pumps six times—once for every strike of the belt. His body is heavy on my burning ass. His thrusts drive my hip bones into the table. His arm reaches around, pulling me impossibly closer, melding our bodies into one.

I feel his forearm tense and his chest and his thighs. His fingers shift to the place where we're joined, and he finds my clit, and he taps it—three sharp blows. He empties into me, groaning one word—*come*—and then he bites me, his teeth closing hard on my neck.

I obey.

I come.

I clutch around him, every muscle tighter than it's ever been before. His pulse is mine. We're sharing one heart, one body, and I cease to exist. I'm never going to be alone again.

Except, after an eternity, I am.

I'm cradled in Trap's lap. His back is braced against one leg of the table. One of his hands rests on my hip. The other caresses the nape of my neck.

Slowly, carefully, I shift my weight. I stretch my legs in front of me. Trap's arms are settled around me, and we spoon, my back to his chest, my head beneath his chin.

He covered me while I was out, pulling my yoga pants over my hips. He loosened his tie from around my wrists. He holds me now, rocking me just a little, back and forth in perfect soothing comfort.

I have to wet my lips before I can speak. Swallow hard. Clear my throat, and even then, my voice is hoarse. "Now I'm confused. Was that the trick? Or the treat?"

His laugh shakes his chest, and his arms tighten around me. He bends down enough to brush his lips against my cheek. "God, I love you."

"I love you too," I say.

And because I love him, I find the strength to stand. I wait for him to climb to his feet too. I lock my knees to keep from swaying. And I settle a hand along his jaw, feeling his steady heartbeat beneath my fingertips. "Get out of here," I say. "Because the sooner you go, the sooner you'll be home again." He starts to say something, but I shake my head. "Now. Go."

And he does.

26

TRAP

So help me Christ, that wasn't what I meant to do.

But here I am, drying off after the world's quickest shower and getting ready to raid my closet for my second-best black pants, black shirt, and black tie. Because while I plan to commit a double kidnapping in a sex club before the night is over, I'm not about to show up smelling like a guy who's already had the best goddamn fuck of his life.

Jesus fucking Christ.

I only meant to bring her candy. I only meant to say I'd see her in the morning. I only meant to give her one kiss before I hit the road, one chance to tell her I love her and everything's going to be okay.

She destroys me.

My entire adult life, I've known I'm a monster. I need things no decent woman should ever allow.

But Alix is the most decent woman I know. And she allows

so much more than I ever dreamed of. She lives for it. Thrives on it.

I was rougher than I meant to be. Her ass will be bruised. Her neck too. I fucking *bit* her.

I'd feel guilty, if I hadn't felt her come harder around me than she's ever come before. I think she actually passed out for a few seconds.

Shit.

I should be feeding her chocolate and making sure she drinks enough water. I should be rubbing salve into her ass. (And no, that's not the invitation my cock seems to think it is.) I should be holding her and helping her come back down and telling her she's everything to me.

Instead, I'll have to prove it another way. I'm going to catch those motherfucking Herzogs and hand them off to Best's men. I'm going to end this fucking war forever.

After tonight, Alix and I will have the rest of our lives to be together. I'll find new ways to make her moan. To make her scream my goddamn name.

Dressed again, I check my pockets for the pair of syringes that will set us free. I've got a thousand bucks with me, but no credit cards, no ID. I don't need car keys, and the house is on biometrics.

Charles is waiting in the freeport parking lot with the Mercedes. He's too professional to note that he expected me almost an hour ago.

"Let's go," I say, after he's taken his place behind the wheel. "Don't worry about making up the time. I can't afford any tickets tonight."

Within minutes, he's on the interstate, keeping a steady pace exactly eight miles above the speed limit. I lean back against the headrest. I spread my hands on my thighs. I try not to wonder what Alix is doing now.

And I wait for the next chapter to begin in our life together.

27

ALIX

I don't start to shake until I'm drying off after my shower. That's when I realize how sore my bottom is. My skin stings like I've got open cuts. My muscles ache like they've been through a grinder.

Maybe it's this bad because I sent Trap away before he could apply his magic salve.

Maybe it's this bad because I let him beat me harder than he's ever done before.

I can't complain. That orgasm truly transported me. Transposed me. Trap turned me into something, someone, I've never been before.

But what the hell does that say about me? Why do I need pain like that to be set free?

I stare at myself in the mirror. I'm a different woman than the tortured creature who arrived at the freeport four months ago. My hair has grown out. I've lost twenty pounds of the weight Herzog forced on me. I've learned how to dress to accommodate my huge breasts, to accentuate them as assets instead of as something that shames me.

But would a healthy woman allow what Trap did to me tonight?

I know all the arguments. I've repeated them to myself so often, I literally recite them in my sleep. They're the soundtrack to my dreams, a slow steady chant of everything I believe.

Trap gives me a safeword. I'm in control. Everything we do is by my choice, with my permission. No matter what we say in the middle of a game, I'm the one in charge.

But what if Klaus Herzog broke something in my brain? What if he and his brothers and all the special guests destroyed some key circuit? What if I'm so damaged I can't even recognize all the ways I'm broken?

All those questions boil down to one: What would my life be like now if Leo had never sold me to Herzog?

Leo.

Leo.

Leo.

It always comes back to Leo.

I'm halfway to Swallowtail Cottage before I realize I'm holding the candy bars Trap gave me. I must have brought them as protection. As some sort of offering. A disguise.

Because I no longer know how to talk to my brother without hiding behind something.

He's been on the freeport grounds for more than two weeks, and this is the first time I've forced myself to visit him. When I think of him wearing clothes paid for by Trap, sleeping in a bed outfitted by Trap, eating food provided by Trap, all I can think of is the freeport gallery I prepared instead.

Leo would be halfway through his captivity by now. Halfway to his scheduled death, if unregulated detox hadn't done the job. Halfway to the end I wrote for him.

And part of me—a slimy, stinking, shameful part—still

wishes I had my revenge. Because that's another thing Herzog took from me forever—my utterly unshakable love for my twin.

Besides, Leo knows me better than any human being on the face of the earth. He'll take one look at my face and know I've been shattered. He'll see that I've sold myself to Trap. He'll know I crushed Bart Carver, destroying the man through blackmail when Trap already had him neutered. Leo will know I'm damned, that there's no coming back from the hell I live in. The old Alix Key is lost forever.

"Trick or treat?" I ask as he opens the door. I could have used my freeport credentials to enter the cottage. My ID is keyed to work the locks, to give me full access to every corner of the freeport except clients' private galleries. But I hold out the bag and show off my collection of treats instead.

Leo stares at me like we're strangers. It's been three weeks since my last visit to Dover General. I relied on Trap's endless stream of chauffeurs and assistants and personal shoppers to get my brother settled in his new life.

But after a long, slow beat, Leo shakes his head and says, "I don't think that's the way Halloween is supposed to work." He steps aside, holding the door open and gesturing me in.

Glancing around, I see he isn't exactly roughing it. The kitchen sparkles with new appliances. An overstuffed couch faces a television the size of Texas. Looking down the hall, I get a glimpse of a high bed jumbled with pillows.

The smell of popcorn is overwhelming. "Did you make enough for me?" I ask, nodding toward the puffy bag that looks like it just came out of the microwave.

"That's my dinner," Leo whines, and we could be hanging out in Candace's kitchen, studying for the SATs all over again.

"And I brought dessert," I remind him, shaking the bag of candy bars. I should tell him he needs to eat more than popcorn. His wrists are thin enough that I could circle them with my thumb and index finger. But it's Halloween, and my brother and I have traditions.

Which Leo clearly remembers, because he's taking two bowls out of the cupboard. "Coke?" he asks, but he's already opening the refrigerator. He pops the top on two cans, pouring them over ice in tall glasses.

I nod toward the TV. "Any chance you get movies on that thing?"

He grins, and for just a moment, he looks like the little boy I grew up with. "There's a movie monster marathon. *Frankenstein* starts in five minutes."

"Then what are we waiting for?"

Leo and I watched *Frankenstein* every Halloween when we were kids. We'd come in from trick-or-treating and take over the coffee table in front of the TV, saying the dialog along with the movie while we engaged in high-stakes candy negotiations. I could wrangle two Snickers for every Reese's Peanut Butter Cup; Leo liked them that much.

Now, my brother flops onto the couch, stretching his legs in front of him and balancing his bowl of popcorn on his chest. His feet are bare, and I remember how filthy they were when Trap brought him to the gallery. Leo's soles are pink now, but I can see thick callouses on his heels and toes.

Just like I can see the scar on his right cheek, the white ring where someone burned him. And I can see his poorly healed broken nose. He used to snore when we were kids, but he outgrew it. I wonder if he has trouble breathing at night now.

Telling myself not to stare, I sit at the other end of the couch. I move a lot more gingerly than Leo does. My butt really hurts from the lashes Trap gave me. I shift a few times, unable to find a comfortable position.

If Leo notices, he doesn't say a word. Instead, he stares at the TV like he's just been brought to life by his own lightning strike. He shovels popcorn into his mouth by the fistful.

I think about Trap. Has he made it out of Delaware yet? Is the traffic bad on the New Jersey Turnpike? What if there's an accident? Will the cops arrest him if they find the syringes in his pocket?

A slow ache leaks behind my eyes. I rub my temples, trying to make it go away.

"It's alive!" Leo shouts.

I'm startled, missing my cue as the monster awakens on the evil doctor's table. Leo shoots me a sideways glance; we're supposed to say the lines together. Whatever he sees in my face makes him study me even closer.

"What?" I ask, blushing. I wonder if he can guess what Trap and I did in the gallery.

"Nothing," he says, but his eyes narrow.

His hair is so short I can still see the tracks of scars on his scalp. Put a couple of bolts on his neck, and he could be the monster on the TV.

Things don't end well for the creature in the movie.

Once again, I think about all the plans I had for my brother, the table he was strapped to, the room I'd prepared to hold him for weeks. He doesn't know what I meant to do. He has no idea how I planned to torture him. The ache behind my eyes starts to pulse in time with my heartbeat.

"Hey," I say, digging into his ribs with my elbow. "Pause the movie. I need to go potty."

Potty. Like we're five years old.

Leo looks at me like I'm nuts. I realize the monster on TV is about to kill its first victim. It's weird for me to take a break now.

Well, this entire night is weird. The man I love is heading north to murder our enemies. I'm pretending like the last three years never happened. I'm half-blind from the headache lancing the backs of my eyes.

Leo runs his hands through his too-short hair, but he picks up the remote and pauses the movie. "Down the hall," he says. "Through the bedroom."

I suck air through my teeth as I stand, countering the throb of my bruised bottom. "Don't even think about touching the Snickers," I say, nodding toward the bag of candy.

"Yeah, yeah, yeah," he grumbles, but he grins.

Leo's bed is unmade, which isn't a surprise. He's left a couple of T-shirts on the floor, tangled with some underwear. In the bathroom, streaks of toothpaste paint the sink. The toilet seat is up.

I close the lid and start to sit down, but my butt reminds me to avoid the hard surface. Instead, I stand in front of the mirror. I take my phone out of my pocket, to see if Trap has left a message. Of course he hasn't. Trap doesn't have his phone. He doesn't have anything that will identify him, in case something goes horribly, drastically wrong.

Squeezing my eyes shut, I tell myself not to picture the pink scar on Trap's biceps, the gunshot wound he got retrieving Leo. I don't want to imagine what could happen to him tonight. How much worse it might be.

My headache marches down my spine. Shoving my phone back in my pants, I open the medicine cabinet, looking for something to beat back the pain.

There's a bottle of Advil, just what I need. Behind it—almost blocked by a tube of toothpaste, by a razor, by a box of Band-Aids—is a plastic bag. I recognize the tiny slips of paper inside. Each one has a cartoon drawing of an explosion and a bright red word: Crash.

As I stare, vomit rises in the back of my throat. I swallow hard and grip the sink. I force myself to take deep breaths, because I honestly believe I might faint.

Crash. Herzog's drug. The one he designed to target children. The one Leo was packing in the Philadelphia warehouse. The one Herzog dosed me with, the night he and his brothers broke me.

It can't be here. Leo is clean. Leo was discharged from the hospital just two weeks ago. He's been at the freeport the whole time. He has no dealer, no way to supply his addiction.

But none of that matters. Because the Crash is here.

I pinch the corner of the slick plastic bag like I'm picking up a dead mouse. I don't bother with the Advil, don't fake-flush the toilet, don't do any of the things I meant to do in the bathroom. I leave the medicine cabinet door open like it needs to be fumigated.

Leo's getting himself another Coke when I walk into the kitchen. "Ready for ano—" He sees what I'm holding. "What the fuck, Al?"

"You're using."

He looks like a rat trapped in a cage. "I'm not!"

"Don't lie to me."

I see him start to make up a story. I can read it in every line of his body, in the set of his jaw, in the way his eyes refuse to meet mine.

"Don't. Lie. To. Me," I repeat, pounding each syllable hard.

He deflates. "You don't understand."

"Where did you even get this stuff?" My voice is an octave too high.

"From one of the orderlies, at the hospital. I'm just maintaining, you know? Only a tab a day."

"A tab a..." I want to scream. I want to scratch his eyes out. I want to rip the shirt off his back and smash his phone on the floor and drag him through the woods to the freeport's front gate.

I want to cry.

"How did you afford it?" I ask. He doesn't have any money. That's one way I knew he was safe.

His face flushes. He's embarrassed. "I traded some of that shit in the hospital room. The Xbox. That crystal clock."

"Leo..." I can't think of anything else to say.

"Crash just makes sense," he says. "It's the only thing that makes me right."

"Makes you *right*?" I shout in disbelief.

And that shuts him down. His face locks into a too-familiar glare. His lips thin. His chin juts.

This is the Leo who refused to talk to our father. The one who ignored my friends' good-intentioned efforts to intervene. The liar who denied, over and over and over again, that he ever needed rehab.

"It's poison," I say, barely keeping my voice even.

"*You* took it," he says, sounding like a child.

"Herzog *forced* me to. You know—Klaus Herzog? The man you sold me to? The man who made me his slave?"

"I made a mistake!" he shouts. "I'm sorry!"

"Sorry," I snort.

"What do you want me to say, Al? He gave me a choice, and I believed him. He'd keep you three days or he'd kill me. I'd give anything to go back to that night! I'd give anything to keep you safe. Don't you know that? Don't you know that every single morning, I wake up wishing I was *dead*?"

"Keep using this crap, and you will be," I say.

"Fine," he says, swiping for the bag, which I hold just out of his reach. "Give it to me. I'll take it all now. I'll OD on your precious boyfriend's hardwood floor, and then you'll never have to worry about me again."

"Shut up," I say, like we're five years old and fighting over who gets to push the button on the elevator.

"That's what you want," he sulks.

"You wouldn't know what I want if it bit you on your fu—freaking ass."

His laugh is nasty. "You hypocritical bitch."

"What?" He measured out every syllable, and it feels like I've been slapped.

"Miss Goody Two-Shoes. Can't say the word fuck? But you're not so innocent now." His voice drips with sarcasm, acid carving every word.

"What are you *talking* about?"

"I take Crash," he says. "I'm an addict. I fucked up my life, and I fucked up yours, and I fucked up a bunch of other people too. I admit it. All of it. But at least I'm not lying."

"I'm not—"

"You fuck that gorilla like the two of you are going for gold in the Kinky Sex Olympics, but you still pretend you're cleaner than the Virgin Mary."

"Leave Trap out of this!"

"Why don't we sit down and talk some more," my brother sneers. "Wait. What? You can't sit? Let me guess. He beat your ass tonight. He left you black and blue, and that's why you've been squirming on that couch like the cushions are on fire."

"You don't know anything about—"

"He bit your fucking neck, Al! And you're *defending* him! I may take Crash, but I don't lie about it. And I don't let a monster use me. I'm not whoring myself out for a new phone and a million-dollar—"

I slap him. My open hand crashes into his face with enough force to send him staggering back three full steps. A thousand bees sting themselves to death on my palm as I run out of Swallowtail Cottage.

28

TRAP

I'm gripping a tumbler in one hand, keeping the other in my pocket, wrapped around the syringes. My glass holds something that used to be Scotch on the rocks, but the ice melted over an hour ago, leaving me with muddy, charcoal-scented water. If I put it down, someone might try to shake my hand, and that would shove the Beast into hyperdrive. The animal in my skull is already rumbling like a volcano about to erupt, growling about how it wants to shred my brain into cat food.

Rider kept his word. The name Kent Clark got me past the front desk. I've already made three slow circuits around the club, lingering as long as I dare by the private room near the back. A small sign by the door says *Reserved.* Bottles of vintage champagne sink in their ice buckets. Molded chocolate truffles gleam under the dim lights, painted to look like raspberries and strawberries and honeybees.

There's no sign of the fucking Herzogs.

A security guard gives me the stink eye, so I take another

cruise around Kynk. Most of the costumes are far more elaborate than my own black mask.

I can't figure out how that mermaid got to the couch where the minotaur is fucking her tits; her tail is too tight to let her take a single step, and she's far too large for one man to carry. The body paint on the skeleton by the bar gives all new meaning to the word boner. I'm pretty sure the snake wrapped around the woman in the corner is real, but I don't want to get close enough to know for sure.

A couple lingers by the table near the door. They're both completely naked. He's got a dog leash clipped to his Prince Albert, and she's telling him to heel while she scans the room like she's looking for a puppy playmate.

In this company, those assless chaps aren't worth a second look, but the butt-plug dangling a floor-length rainbow tail gets some attention. Club rules say no one can ask the woman wearing the colossal strap-on for her autograph, even if she's starring in that Broadway revival of *The Sound of Music.*

"Look like you could use a fresh drink." I turn away from the circle jerk of guys wearing kilts to see Gage Rider's wry smile. He's wearing a plain black tuxedo, which stands out in this crowd like a buck-naked priest on Christmas Eve.

I let him order me a replacement, raising the glass after he tells the bartender to pour the MacAllan 18. "You're not drinking?" I ask.

"I'm working. Keeping an eye on the crowd." His grin is easy as he looks away from a pair of women dressed as sex dolls. If the heavy lipstick circling their mouths turns him off as much as it does me, he doesn't give a sign.

"Speaking of crowd," I say. "Any chance you've seen our friends?"

"Not yet," he says. "They're usually here by nine."

There isn't a clock in sight, but it has to be after midnight. "Any chance they've taken a different private room?"

Rider nods to a guy in a diaper. "They'd still have to come

through the front door. I just talked to Lydia. They haven't checked in."

Fuck.

"You think they heard a fan wanted to meet them?"

Rider's negative shake is sharp. "I'm the only one who knew you'd be able to make it."

"Anyone else have scores to settle?"

"Against those guys? Probably hundreds. But vengeful motherfuckers like that won't get past my front door. What sort of club do you think I'm running here?"

A woman walks by in classic dominatrix gear, ignoring the man behind her who's whining, "Please, Mistress. Unlock my cock cage for just thirty seconds…"

Before I can answer Rider, he presses his fingers against an almost-invisible earpiece. "Put him in holding room one. I'll be there in a minute."

Adrenaline spikes the base of my brain. "One of our guys?"

Rider shakes his head. "Just someone…very high up in the mayor's office. Upset that his mask got pulled off in one of the private rooms."

"Good luck with that," I say.

He takes one more look around the room. "I don't have to warn you to be careful, do I?"

"You just did. And no."

He swaggers through the crowd, cutting a swath wide enough for two men to follow in his wake.

I want to believe the Herzogs are just late arrivals. Maybe they got tied up handing out candy to neighborhood kids. They could be delayed by a hyper-competitive bobbing-for-apples contest.

But in my gut, I know they aren't coming.

Nevertheless, I take another circuit around the club. It's getting late. The initial frenzy of the party guests has died down, and a lot of people are just standing around and talking. In fact,

I don't see any real action until I reach the large room at the back.

A stage is framed by a bright spotlight. A Dom sits on a hard wooden chair, his little blonde sub balanced over his lap. She's dressed in a classic schoolgirl outfit, plaid mini-skirt, white top that shows half her tits, her hair in braids. Her skirt's flipped up, and her ass is bright red. She's begging, "Please, Daddy, please." From the sound of her squeal as he spanks her again, she's about one smack away from coming.

I'm staring at her ass, but I'm not seeing it. I'm listening to her moan, but I'm not hearing her. I'm back in Dover, back at the freeport, standing over Alix with my belt in my hand.

She wanted it. She begged me for it. If it was too much, if I gave her more than she bargained for, she would have used her safeword.

But she didn't safeword here, when she was with Jonas and Ansel, surrounded by a crowd of curious party guests. She let those cumrags bind her tight enough to dislocate a less limber woman's shoulders. She let them gag her with a tool she hates. She let them draw blood with a cane.

I know the argument. Rider's security guard choked it into me: Alix didn't set a safeword. The club wasn't responsible for stopping the Herzogs because Alix exercised her own free will.

But was she truly free to act that night? Was she in her right mind? Or was her past with Jonas and Ansel simply too overwhelming?

And what about tonight? Did I take things too far? Was Alix capable of telling me when to stop?

She trusts me. That's why what we have works. I respect her one hard limit: no anal. And everything else, she draws the line —if it hurts too much... If it dredges up nightmares... Hell if she'd just rather curl up with her stuffed panda and watch stupid videos on her phone for the night.

She's the one in charge.

She's safeworded before. But when was the last time she

stopped me? What if she's forgotten how? What if Jonas and Ansel broke her here, and I've been too blind or too horny or too fucking confident that I'm the man she needs?

The little blonde is coming now, putting on a show, bucking and screaming and peeking out at the crowd to make sure everyone appreciates how hard she's working. I turn and push my way out of the room.

I barely waste time in the Green Room, pulling on my shirt. I make Charles pull the car around the corner, and I get out to tell Best's guys the deal is off. I toss the syringes in a storm drain as I get back in the Mercedes, and I tell Charles to hurry, to get us home. I don't give a fuck about John Law.

I just need to get to Alix.

29

ALIX

I don't know how I get from Swallowtail Cottage back to the house. I'm crying as I stumble down the path in the woods, and I can't catch my breath. Part of my brain is chanting, "Trap, Trap, Trap..." and I want him and I need him and I can't have him because he's in New York getting the Herzogs out of our lives forever.

But even as I long for his arms around me, for his stern commands, for the absolute certainty that he loves me as much as I love him, I hear my brother's nasty sneer: *I don't let a monster use me.*

As I tumble into Trap's house, I know my brother is right. I've whored myself out for a security system that will keep me safe from the nightmares that stalk the real world. I've spread my legs for the fifty-dollar bottle of water I gulp in the kitchen. I've traded my last shred of self-respect for the phone I check, looking for a message from Trap before I remember once again that he left his phone behind.

Folding my arms around my belly, I pace our bedroom. I can't help but look at the bed's iron headboard, at the footboard where I've been bound too many times to count. The tall dresser glares at me, daring me to open the bottom drawer. A pile of clothes slumps by the closet like a body, and I realize they're the pants and shirt Trap wore when he said goodbye in the gallery.

He fucked me. He bound my hands with his necktie. He beat my ass with his belt. He pushed his cock into my pussy from behind and he pumped and he pumped and I let him, because I'd do anything for Trap—just the way he taught me.

Leo is right. I *am* a hypocrite.

My legs are shaky. How long have I been walking this path —bed to dresser to closet to bed? I glance at the clock on the nightstand. Impossibly, it's 12:17.

Halloween is over. Trap should have dealt with the Herzogs by now. He should be back in the car with Charles. He should have access to a phone; he should be able to let me know he's safe.

What if he's not?

What if the Herzogs set a trap for him? What if they fought back? What if the Mercedes was T-boned by a drunk driver, and Trap was thrown into a filthy Brooklyn gutter?

If Trap is lying in a hospital bed, I don't have any right to see him. We're not family. I'm not his wife.

If a doctor asked, I have no idea what Trap would want—how long he'd stay on a ventilator, whether surgeons should take heroic measures. I don't even know if he has a will.

1:08.

I'm getting way ahead of myself. Trap must be fine. Gage would have called if anything happened at the club. The police would be at the freeport gates if there'd been an accident.

Gage is a freeport client. He doesn't have my personal phone number. He has no way to reach me.

Trap left the house without any ID. How long will that delay my getting news?

1:22.

I'm exhausted. I'm terrified. Every muscle in my body aches—not just the bruises Trap left, but my arms, my legs, even the bones of my fingers.

I'm still clutching Leo's plastic bag. All this time, I've been gripping it, like I can hold onto my brother, hold onto Trap, hold onto everything in my crazy, screwed-up world.

The little slips of paper mock me with their cartoon bombs, their explosions and the word: Crash.

The only time I've taken Crash—taken any street drug—was when Herzog forced two tabs past my O-ring gag. Even as I was triple-teamed by all three Herzog brothers, I thought the Crash was the worst violation of my body.

It raped my soul. It made me complicit in my brother's addiction, in what I thought at the time was my brother's death.

But I was wrong.

Crash saved me. The drug numbed me. It took me away from the barbaric things those men did to my body. It kept me safe when I could no longer protect myself. It saved my sanity.

Is that what Crash does for Leo? Is that why he can't leave it behind, no matter how much I've begged, no matter what it's cost him?

All these years, I've fought to change my brother. I've paid for him to go to rehab. I've given him a place to stay when he comes back to the real world. I've fended off all the people who weren't willing to give him another chance.

But I've never truly understood him.

Crash! say the little pieces of paper.

Where the hell is Trap? What will I do if he's gone forever?

I want to go to Leo. I want to say I get it now. If Crash can take away this terror, this pain, only a fool would pass it up.

There's no way Leo will open the cottage door to me. I don't dare use my freeport ID to force my way in. Leo knew what he said tonight would knife me to the core. He knew he'd destroy me. But he said it anyway, because it's the truth. Because it's *me*, in a way I couldn't see.

1:42.

The plastic bag feels like satin beneath my fingers. Each piece of paper is a slip of lost dreams. I choose one at random. I stare at the little explosion, bracing myself for how it will detonate in my brain.

When I put it on my tongue, I expect an instant reaction. I brace for a flood of salt or maybe sour, for bitter or sickening sweet. I wait for my fingers to tingle, for my breath to come fast and shallow, for my heart to shift into overdrive.

But there's nothing. Just a thicker gob of spit that slides down my aching throat.

Five minutes pass with no change, and I wonder if the Crash is even real. Maybe the papers are a joke, some twisted game the hospital orderly played on a vulnerable patient. Maybe Leo only thinks this bag *makes him right*. The placebo effect—I know all about it from grad school.

I sit on the bed and open my nightstand drawer. There's a nail file in there and a small pair of scissors. Hand lotion and a stray bookmark. A bottle of lube.

I shove the plastic bag all the way to the back. I'll give it back to Leo tomorrow. Bring him a Reese's Peanut Butter Cup as a peace offering. See if we can start over. Again.

My fingers slip off the nightstand drawer as I try to close it. My hand has turned to lead; it's almost too heavy for me to lift. I have to concentrate, using all my willpower to force the drawer closed.

I'm thirsty. I need a glass of water. My feet, though, are miles from the floor. The bathroom is a continent away.

I force myself to make the trek, holding on to furniture and the walls. The water is so cold it turns my bones to ice. My glass fills with music—something I've heard before, but I can't remember where. It's the soundtrack to a dream.

When I look in the mirror, my eyes are huge. They're all

pupil, all black; no one would ever know my driver's license says they're brown.

The water tastes like moonlight. I drink a full glass, and then another, and each sip frees a different note deep inside my brain.

I was worried about something, but I can't remember what. I was afraid, but there was no reason. I need someone, no, something…

I need music. I run my fingers under the tap, splashing to make sounds I've never heard before. I hold my breath so I don't miss a note.

The song weaves into my bones. It reshapes my organs. It turns me inside out, making every cell in my body a separate, perfect instrument.

I follow the notes back to the bed. The sheets play a secret concert against my skin. My pillow whispers a symphony. Every time I turn my head, I'm suspended on new sounds I can't describe.

I turn off the light. I close my eyes. I hold my breath. And the music carries me deeper and deeper into my brain, until I can pluck individual neurons and lose myself in the music of my soul.

30

TRAP

Alix is sound asleep when I get home. I shouldn't be surprised; it's after three in the fucking morning, and that's with Charles collecting a three-hundred-dollar speeding ticket on the goddamn Jersey Turnpike. The officer wanted to run us in for reckless driving, but a thousand bucks convinced him to write it down to thirty-nine above the posted limit.

The water is running in the bathroom, which is weird, but maybe Alix needed the white noise to help her fall asleep. I shuck off my clothes, adding them to the pile I left before I hit the road. I'm already reaching to spoon her when I climb into bed.

She's throwing off heat like a campfire, which only makes me realize my hands and feet are blocks of ice. For one heartless second, I think about where I can plant them, to wake her up quick. I'm a fucking gentleman, though. I rub my palms together, using friction to thaw my fingers. I keep my toes to myself.

When I cup my hands around her gorgeous tits, her nipples peak at my first touch. She moans in her sleep, but she pushes back against me. My cock registers its approval.

I take the lobe of her ear between my teeth, biting just hard enough to make that gorgeous sound ripple from her throat again. Without opening her eyes, she says, "It sounds like starlight."

She's dreaming. I should let her sleep. But she's pressing her back against me, and I'm so fucking wired, and the only way I can stop playing with her tits is to test the furnace between her legs.

She's wet. Soaking. Like she just beat off minutes ago, and now she's drifting in the afterglow.

I shift her leg to a better angle and push in hard. A smile teases her lips. With her eyes still closed, she says, "Listen. Hush."

But I'm not listening. And she's not staying hushed. I'm used to my princess chanting my name; I've learned her exact change of pitch when she's close to coming. But this is the first time I've ever heard her *sing* as I fuck her.

It starts as a hum, a buzz that vibrates from her throat to her back. That sound ripens into a moan. The faster I stroke, the higher her tone, each note drawn out into something weird and strange and fucking irresistible. It's like my cock is playing her, like she's some sort of instrument I've never heard before in my life.

I get lost in the music. I don't have to tell her I fucked up at the club. I don't have to admit the Herzogs are still out there. We'll never be free.

For this moment in time, in this separate space, it's just Alix and me, finding some new way to lose our minds in and around and for each other.

I slow down because I don't want to lose this. Once I blow my wad, it's going to be Alix and me, back to normal. I'll have to tell her everything that happened at Kynk. Everything that didn't.

But she's getting closer. I can feel it in the tightness of her ass. Her breath is coming shorter, breaking up her crazy song. Her skin is slick with sweat, sliding against mine like we're one machine.

I reach around to find her clit with my fingers. I open my mouth to give her the command she needs. I'm ready to tell her to come, ready to push hard one last time, to bury my cock in her heat as she pulses fast around me.

Before I can say it, though, before I can set her free, she finds a new note. It's steady and it's low, back to the hum that started this strange fuck, but she holds it and she holds it and she holds it and the whole time she's singing, she's coming around my cock.

It's not like when I tell her what to do. She doesn't seize hard like a wild animal breaking out of her cage. Instead, she... collapses. She drifts away like sand running out of a timer. Her humming fades away, and I swear to God she's fallen back asleep.

I pump a few more times. My cock is still a needy bastard, but my brain says I'm breaking some sort of rule.

I pull out and finish myself with my hand. Alix barely stirs as my cum splashes onto her back.

It's weird, that's what it is. It's goddamn strange.

But every fuck can't be a decathlon gold medal. It's four in the goddamn morning. I fucked up at Kynk, and the shitstains I thought I'd kill tonight are still on the loose.

I can't imagine the emotional toll on Alix as she sat at home, waiting, wanting news that we're free, afraid to hear that I was hurt. Or worse.

We both came, so what's my fucking problem?

I get a warm washcloth and clean her up enough that I don't feel like a total jackass. She's still throwing off heat like a blast furnace. I slip the sheet over her shoulders, and then I head into the guest room to get a couple of hours of sleep before the freeport screams for my attention.

31

ALIX

I wake feeling like my skull's been cracked open and my brain has been left to rot on a sidewalk. Every muscle in my body aches. My mouth stinks like a sewer.

I'm still trying to find the will to move when a rusty door groans open inside my mind.

Trap was here. Trap came home. He came back from Kynk, and I was too far gone to talk to him. To ask him what happened. To find out if Jonas and Ansel are finally, finally gone.

I was a waste, because I took Leo's Crash.

A cold wash of shame floods my body in slow motion, starting at the crown of my head and ending at my toenails. Trap risked his *life* for us, and I got high in our bed.

My memory is patchy. Trap's hands were on my breasts. I sang him the song inside my head, the notes I'd never heard before. We made love, or we tried to. I couldn't move. Couldn't find my way out of the music.

I don't think I orgasmed. No. Wait. That's not right. I did, but it wasn't the same. It wasn't the way Trap makes me feel.

It was like a hiccup.

A sneeze.

Was it good for Trap at least? I don't remember him swearing. I missed his usual flood of filthy words, his raw, unfiltered thoughts as our bodies set each other free.

I don't remember waking once during the night. Hearing him breathing beside me. Feeling his heat against my back.

I sit on the edge of the bed, gulping deep breaths and trying not to puke. Stakes pound into the base of my skull. My bones grind to dust inside me.

I need to find Trap. Find out what happened at Kynk. Make sure he's okay.

My feet can't find the floor. Somehow, I end up sitting beside the bed, my legs splayed in front of me. My body aches like one gigantic bruise.

I try to crawl to the bathroom, but I'm too weak. I call out, hoping Trap will hear me, but no one answers. I start to cry, but it takes too much energy to sob, so I just let the tears leak out of my eyes.

I can't stay here. I need to move. I need to get to the freeport office tower, to find Trap.

A flurry of notes whispers from my nightstand drawer. The song is soft, like I'm hearing it from miles away. But I know that tune. It's the music of my soul. It's sweet, sweet salvation.

I remember shoving the bag to the back of the drawer. I can feel the plastic beneath my fingers, smooth and cool. I can picture the slips of paper inside, bright and cheerful, with their funny little cartoon drawing.

Just one square. I can let it dissolve on my tongue. It will drive away the weakness, push back the pain.

Once I can stand on both feet, I can make a plan. I can figure out how to taper off the Crash. I'll take half a dose tomorrow, a quarter the next day, and then everything will be back to normal.

The song ratchets up in my head as I open the drawer. It fills my entire body as I work open the slider on the bag. It floods over me, around me, *through* me as that tiny square of paper dissolves on my desperate tongue.

It only takes a few minutes for me to become human. I shower, wrapped in music. I dress, clothed in song. And I hide the plastic bag of Crash in the guest room so no one will worry about what I've done.

If I eat, I can manage the Crash. Food in my stomach buffers the drug. I still have the music, still have the song, but I can walk and talk and think like a normal human being.

And with cheese and an apple under my belt, I realize my bottom doesn't hurt nearly as much. I can sit on one of the stools in the kitchen without squirming. I don't need to finger the bruise on my neck either, the dark purple circle from Trap's teeth.

I wear a turtleneck when I head over to the freeport. It's November. No one will be suspicious.

Susan is coming out of Trap's office just as I get there. "Careful," she says in a low voice. "*Someone* is in a mood."

But the Crash whistles a few notes deep in my head. I know how to handle Trap, bad mood or not. "Thanks for the warning," I say.

Trap's on the phone when I close the door behind me. It's a burner, and he's talking too fast. Or maybe my ears are hearing too fast. "Your men did their job," he says. "Not their fault if the cocksuckers hid under rocks."

He listens for a moment, his face growing dark. Then he says, "If I *knew* where they were, I wouldn't have sat around the club half the night with my thumb up my ass."

Another reply. Trap says, "Very funny. You should take that show on the fucking road." A quick pause, and then, "Let me know if anyone goes in or out. We're close. I can feel it."

When the call ends, Traps looks at me and shrugs. "Best's turned into some sort of comedian. Says there were a lot better things I could do at Kynk than sit on my own fucking thumb."

The music distracts me, and I miss the chance to laugh. Instead I say, "Sorry I was out of it when you got home."

He gestures with the burner. "You got the gist. Jonas and Ansel didn't show. Best is keeping an eye on the Long Island house."

More music. But I remember to shrug and say, "We've waited this long…"

"I don't like the fact that no one knows where they are."

My chest feels tight. Maybe I don't like that either. Before I can say anything, though, the music swells. It washes away my anxiety, like Jonas and Ansel Herzog were just a bad dream.

"Hey," Trap says. "Are you okay?"

"Why wouldn't I be?"

"Your face looks flushed. And you were burning up when I got into bed last night."

I shove down the music because I know how to make this right. I cross the office. I take the burner out of Trap's hand and put it on his desk. I start to close the distance between us, to slip my arms around his neck, to pull him close for a kiss that echoes the notes in my head. But before my lips find his, his desk phone rings, on the intercom's private line.

Trap lowers his forehead to mine, taking a long, deep breath that seems to steady him. "I swear to God, I'm going to rip out that line and let Susan shout at me from her desk."

The music doesn't like the words *rip* or *shout*. It slips into muddy chords, into something that sounds like danger. But I know how to fix that too.

Trap's already on the phone as I reach the door. I wave and head back to the house.

I was right. I *did* know how to drown out those ugly discords. Another slip of paper, dissolved on my tongue in the guest room, turns all the music bright again.

Even when I think about Jonas and Ansel Herzog, somewhere they can't be tracked.

Even when I think about Trap, overburdened with the freeport and the Herzogs and me.

Even when I think about Leo, who will probably never speak to me again after I slapped him, after I took his Crash.

The music plays on and on, and I close my eyes, the better to hear the individual notes.

32

TRAP

I can broker deals worth millions of dollars.

I can manage egos, making billionaires stand in line like naughty little children.

I can drop half a dozen opponents in the krav maga gym, even when they come at me in pairs, in trios.

But I can't figure out how to talk to Alix.

I shouldn't be surprised that she's giving me the cold shoulder. I can only imagine how hard she had to work, getting her head around what I planned to do at Kynk.

Forget that I went to a sex club. She trusts me. She knows about my Beast. She knows I'll never fuck another woman behind her back.

But the club is filled with traumatic memories for her. Plus, she—of all people—knows how much murder weighs.

I was supposed to take out the men who raped her, and I failed.

I failed, and then I came home and fucked her, which wasn't the most brilliant idea my dick has ever had.

I'll be honest. There will never be a time I can't get it up for Alix Key. But the last few nights, I've made sure to work late at the office. I've taken business calls from Tokyo and Seoul and Singapore. I've headed up to Wilmington for a Chamber of Commerce meeting. I've gone on long runs, like I'm training for a fucking marathon.

Because there was something off that night, when I got home.

Alix came without me telling her to. I can justify that. I can tell myself stories. And I can come up with games for us to play, a little discipline to get her back in line, things I know she'll melt for.

But part of my lizard brain is afraid it just won't work.

So it's easier to be busy than to take care of business. It's easier to pretend everything's fine in the world. In the freeport. In my bed.

And here's the kicker: Alix doesn't come looking for me. She sleeps in the guest room. She stares at her phone. She's just as happy with me out of the house.

I've lost her.

And I don't know how to turn that around.

33

ALIX

This is how Leo has lived for years. All this time, I thought he was weak, that he was broken. But now I understand.

The Crash has opened parts of my brain that have always been locked away.

Here's the secret I learn, one week into taking Crash: the music is my angel. She first came to me in Herzog's study. She showed me how to leave my body when Herzog and his brothers hurt me. She fed me strawberries that tasted like diamonds, and she sang to me.

The music is her voice. The music is my angel folding me in her wings and keeping me safe in a world that holds men like the Herzog brothers.

And now that I've found her again, now that I know she's always here around me, I'll never leave her again.

That's why I stop going to my office, over in the freeport tower. I don't want to fill my brain with computer messages and ringing telephones and dozens of people talking about meaningless business details.

And that's why I stop going to my gallery, to the library Trap gave me. All the paintings I could ever want live inside my mind now. The angel paints them for me, using colors I've never seen before. She sings them into my soul, remapping my cells to match her designs.

And that's why I move into the guest room. Now, I can stay awake all night, without disturbing Trap. I can walk through the windows with my angel. We can travel to the stars and back, without bothering a soul.

Once, I tell my angel I should speak to Trap. I should tell him where we're going, what we're doing, what I'm finally able to see and hear. But the angel tells me he isn't ready. He won't understand. We need to give him time to find his own angel, somewhere down the road.

Another time, I tell my angel we have to go back to Swallowtail Cottage. I have to see Leo. I have to tell him I'm sorry for all the times I tried to stop him, for all the times I tried to keep him from his own private angel.

But every time I think about going to my brother, I remember the slap of my hand against his face. I remember the look of betrayal in his eyes. I remember the pain of what he told me, the truth of his words that cut so deep I almost bled out.

Trap was my drug. He was my reason for living. That wasn't right. It wasn't healthy.

I understand that now, because I have my angel. And I'm never letting her go away again.

34

TRAP

~

Hell is knowing the woman you love would rather sleep in the guest room with her arms around a goddamn stuffed panda than spend a night with you doing…anything.

I tried.

I respected her privacy. I knocked on her door. I didn't invade her space, didn't even turn on the overhead light, just stood ten feet away and acted like everything was perfectly normal.

She didn't want to come down for dinner. She didn't want to drive to Lewes for a midnight walk on the deserted beach. She didn't want to fly to New York, to Boston, to the fucking North Pole.

Every time I suggested something, she just said, "No, thank you. I'd prefer to stay here."

My palms itched to go in there, to throw the bedclothes on the floor, to yank off her sweatpants and that over-size sleep shirt and make her remember everything we have together.

But I told her I understood. I told her if she changed her mind, I'd be downstairs.

And now, it's three hours later, and I'm still staring at my fucking computer screen, trying to remember what I did with an empty evening before Alix.

That's the division of my life now: Before Alix and after Alix.

I'm terrified that the "after" part means something new, that it means after Alix left me. And it's going to stretch forever.

I'm halfway through my second double Pigwhistle when the doorbell rings. My doorbell never rings. I live in the middle of a fucking business park. There's a six-story office tower and a matching underground warehouse. There's a fucking NASCAR-quality racetrack. There's an electrified security fence running the perimeter and guards on duty 24/7. Who the fuck goes door to door?

"Jesus fucking Christ," I mutter when I check the security screen. It's Alix's brother. Leo.

It's a sign of how much I love the woman sleeping in my guest room that I open the fucking door. "What do you want?" I ask.

He puffs up like pigskin dropped in hot oil. It's funny, really. I half expect him to launch at my face, fingernails extended and voice screeching like some kind of shit-throwing monkey.

"Where's Alix?"

"She's sleeping." I don't make any move to let him into the house.

"I need to see her."

"Tough shit. Leave her a message, and she'll go down to the cottage tomorrow."

"I left her a message." *Asshole.* I see him start to say it. I watch him reconsider. Maybe he *isn't* as dumb as he looks. "She didn't answer."

"Then leave her another one."

"I've left her ten. I've been trying to reach her all week."

"Then here's an idea, Einstein. Maybe she doesn't want to talk to you."

He shifts his weight from foot to foot. Rubs his palms against his thighs. Cranes his neck and looks past me into the hall, like maybe Alix is standing right behind me.

This is the rat-fuck who sold Alix to Herzog. Every bone in my body is screaming at me to knock him to the ground. Take a swing at his goddamn face. Maybe break that nose a second time.

But for Alix's sake, I fold my fingers into fists. She wants him at the freeport. I have to live with that. But I sure as hell don't have to invite the dickwad in for tea and cookies.

I think about telling him I'm going upstairs to fuck his sister. Let him know who's boss around here. But that turns Alix into the punchline of a bad joke. And the only thing she's done wrong is have the bad luck to share a birthday with this clown.

"Anything else?" I ask. "Because I have to get back to work."

"Yeah," he says, before I can slam the door in his face. "There *is* something else. Alix took something that belongs to me. I need it back. Now."

"*Alix* took something from *you*?" The scrawny bastard literally didn't have a stitch of clothing when I paid for his suite at the hospital. Everything he owns—from the clothes on his back to the phone shoved in the pocket of his jeans—was a gift from his sister. Which means it was a gift from me.

"Look," he says. "Just let me get it, and I'll be out of your hair."

"I've got another idea, motherfucker. Get off my doorstep, and my *hair* will be just fine."

I never expected the shitbird would lower a shoulder and try to tackle me in my own house. His technique sucks, and I outweigh him almost two to one, but I'm surprised enough to take a step back.

"Alix!" he fucking hollers. "Hey! Alix!"

It would be easy enough to knock him flat on his ass. I might take out a tooth or two with a solid punch to his jaw. I could easily kick him senseless, even though I'm only wearing running shoes.

But he's Alix's goddamn brother. And even if she's ignoring his texts, she'll probably be pissed if I put him back in the hospital.

"Alix!" he shouts one more time before I get him in a headlock.

"Shut the fuck up," I growl, even as the Beast explodes inside my brain. It takes all my willpower not to tap out a five-count with his head against the tile floor. "I said your sister was sleeping. Now get your ass back to the cottage, and when she wakes up, I'll tell her you stopped by."

He's stupid enough to keep fighting. He kicks at the door, slamming it closed. His fingers scratch at my forearm, but he can't get a purchase. I tighten my grip, realizing I'll have to choke out this motherfucker to get him to back down.

"Trap!"

Alix's voice cuts through the Beast howling in my brain. She's standing at the foot of the stairs, blinking in the overhead light like she just climbed out of a cave. Her pupils are the size of fifty-pound free-weight plates.

"Trap," she says again, and this time it sounds like her voice is coming from very far away. It's almost like she's singing, like she's chanting something written in a book. "Let him go," she says.

I give her brother an extra shake, sending him half-way to the wall as I set him free. He's still staggering for balance when I say, "He started it."

But Leo cuts me off before I can tell her I was only trying to make sure she could sleep. "Jesus, Alix," he says. "How much did you take?"

She cocks her head and stares past both of us, like there's someone else in the hall. "I can't say that," she says.

I turn and look behind me, even though I know I'm only

going to see the door. The Beast is still raging for its payment because of that chokehold. But it's not the Beast that makes the hair stand up on the back of my neck. It's the weird sing-song way that Alix says to thin air, "They won't understand."

I round on Leo. "What the fuck did you give her?"

"I didn't give her anything! She took it!"

"What did she take?" I loom over him, forcing him back three steps. His shoulders hit the wall, and there's nowhere else for him to go. The Beast howls, demanding that I punch my way back to sanity. When Leo doesn't come up with an answer, my fist lands right by his ear, emphasizing every word: "What. Did. She. Fucking. Take?"

"Crash!" he whimpers, taking away my target by sliding to the floor. "She stole my stash on Halloween." He looks past my legs and shouts to Alix, "But you didn't get it all! I kept some in my nightstand, just in case. And in my sock drawer, too." As fast as he started yelling, he switches back to whining. "It's all gone now. I need the rest. I need what Alix took."

What the actual fuck? Alix had no reason to take the motherfucker's stash.

But it was Halloween.

I was at Kynk.

Alix was waiting. Alone. Afraid. And when I came home, after I failed, everything was different…

I turn to Alix. "Is he telling the truth?"

She does that freaky thing again, looking past me. She nods, like she's listening to someone I can't hear. And then she says, eyes locked on a point beside the front door, "But if I tell them, they'll take you away."

"Oh my God," Leo says. "You are fucking flying."

He laughs like he's just heard the funniest joke in the world. He sits on my floor, and he leans his head back against the wall, and he howls until he's a snorting, drooling mess. He's as high as she is. I should have realized it sooner, but he's had more years of practice, covering it up.

I want to kick his balls into his fucking brain. I can't, because Alix is watching. She's carrying on an argument with someone I can't see, someone I can't hear.

"Alix," Leo says, when he can finally draw a full breath. "Stick-up-your-ass Alix." I'm still rumbling deep in my chest, deciding if it's worth it to smash his fucking face in, when he calls out to his sister, "So much for saying *your* shit doesn't stink. Want the number of my guy? Ready to hook up with Orderly Feel Good at Dover Gen—"

My foot connects with the point of his chin, snapping his head back so hard I may have broken his neck. No such luck, though. He slumps all the way to the floor, knocked out but breathing.

I've got Security on speed dial. Snatching my phone out of my pocket, I tap the number and snap a command. I just have time to walk Alix into my office and get her seated in one of the leather chairs before the doorbell rings like a fireworks finale on the Fourth of July. She's humming as I close the door, reaching out her hand toward something I can't see.

Security made it in under a minute. When this fucking nightmare is over, I'll give someone a bonus. For now, though, I kick Leo's prone body. "Get this asshole off the property."

The guard stands straight, like a soldier at attention. "Yes, sir!" But then he falters and says, "Where should I take him, sir?"

Drown him in the fucking bay. That's what I want to say. But that probably goes beyond "other duties as assigned".

"Drop him at Dover General," I say. "Leave him in the ER. No need to wait."

"Yes, sir," the guard says. He's impressively efficient at hauling Leo into a fireman's carry. I slam the door on the pair of them and go back to the study.

Alix has slid out of the chair. She's sitting cross-legged on the floor, arms folded around her belly. She's rocking back and forth, singing a tuneless song under her breath, afraid, confused, lost.

Something snaps inside my chest. I sit down beside her. She doesn't react.

"Alix," I say, purposely softening my tone, maybe too much because she doesn't even blink. "Hey," I try again, a little louder. "Princess."

That gets her attention, but only for a moment. Then she's back to her singing, focusing on a point somewhere in the middle distance.

"Who's there?" I ask her. "Are you talking with someone?"

A smile floods her face. She isn't scared anymore. She's happier than I've ever seen her. It's like a massive rainstorm has washed away all the shit in her life—her fuck-up of a brother, her lost family and friends, everything Herzog did to her, what she did to Herzog. She's clean and she's pure and she's safe in a way I've never been able to make her feel.

"It's my angel," she says. "Can't you see my angel?"

"Sure," I say, my throat so tight I think I might die.

"My angel says I'm safe now. My angel says you'll never hurt me."

Thank sweet fucking Jesus for that. "Come on," I say, pushing myself to my feet. I hold out a hand, and there's another little miracle, because she stands beside me.

"Where are we going?"

"You're going to bed now."

"And you?"

"I've got some work to do," I say. "But I'll be here in the morning, when you wake up."

"With my angel!" she says. "We'll both be here with my angel. I'm sorry I didn't tell you about her before. I didn't think you'd like her. I didn't think you'd want her to stay. But that was wrong, wasn't it? I was being silly."

Silly. Like a goddamn helpless child.

"Everything'll be okay now."

"Because you like my angel, right? Because she can stay with us forever and ever?"

"Forever and ever," I say, because the lie makes her walk up the stairs with me. It takes her into our bedroom. It lies down beside her in the bed.

I wait until she's asleep before I toss the fucking guest room. And when I find the bag of Crash, I imagine it's Leo Key's neck, squeezed to death between my fists.

35

ALIX

~

Angel?

I can't hear you, Angel.

Please, don't leave me. I need you. You're the only reason I survived Herzog. Survived his brothers.

It took me so long to find you again. Don't go away now. Don't leave me behind.

Angel?

~

My skin is hot enough to set the sheets on fire.

I'm drenched in sweat, but my heart and lungs are frozen.

I'm shivering so hard my bones are starting to crumble.

My fingernails ache. My teeth ache. My hair aches, all of it so bad I want to cry forever.

But my eyes are too dry for tears.

My mouth is parched.

I'm going to dry up and turn to dust and blow away forever.

~

I never knew a human being could puke as much as I have.

My stomach emptied of food hours ago, days ago, a lifetime ago. I'm left with dry heaves that make my ribs ache.

I'm tired. So tired. I can't stand over the toilet. I can't kneel on the floor.

I can barely press my face against the edge of the plastic bowl and do what the voice says: "Let it go. I've got you. Let it go."

~

They're talking.

I can't open my eyes, but I hear them. They don't know music; they don't sing songs. They're nothing like my angel.

"How much longer will this take?"

"As I told you, Mr. Prince. It's different for every user."

"She was only on it for a week."

"But she took it before."

"Once. Three years ago."

"We've seen this in some patients. The dopamine receptors get primed by the first dose, especially if it was a large one."

"Fucking double dose."

"You have no idea how much she took last week?"

"You think I'm lying, Doctor? Why the *fuck* would I lie?"

"Why don't you get some rest, Mr. Prince? Nurse Weiss will be here overnight."

"I don't need any motherfucking rest. What I *need*—"

"You're disturbing my patient, Mr. Prince. Look at that pulse monitor. If you can't control yourself, I'll have no choice but to—"

"Fine. Fine. I'm sitting down. I'm keeping my voice down."

"Please, Mr. Prince. Just lie down in the room across the hall. Nurse Weiss will call you the instant anything changes."

"I'm staying."

"Mr. Prince—"

"Is my staying going to make her any worse? Am I hurting her by being here?"

"Not if you keep your temper, but—"

"Case closed."

"Very well, Mr. Prince."

There's a long pause. I hear people moving. Someone takes my hand. And then, so quiet I almost can't make it out: "Jesus fucking Christ. Goddamn doctors think they run the motherfucking world."

It's not my angel. But it's a song all the same. I fall asleep with someone holding my hand.

I open my eyes, but the sun is so bright I need to close them again. Tears squeeze out between my lashes.

"There you are, Beautiful." It's a woman's voice. A kind voice. A voice that I realize I've heard, off and on for days.

"H— H—" I can't make myself say a word.

She holds something to my lips. A straw. "There you go. A little water will clear that throat right up."

I swallow. The water is ice-cold and it feels like magic. "Hello," I manage on my third try. And then, because it's the most important thing I can ask, I say, "Trap?"

"Mr. Prince is downstairs getting coffee. He'll be back in just a moment."

"Wh— who..."

"I'm Nurse Allen. I'm your daytime nurse."

"How l— long..."

"You've been sleeping for a while. Ten days. Even Dr.

Hanson was starting to get a little worried. If Mr. Prince had called her when this started…"

My eyes well up. Ten days.

I can remember bits and pieces. Losing my angel. Trap holding my head while I was sicker than I've ever been in my life. Trap talking to someone… Dr. Hanson, I guess. Trap muttering his filthy words like a mantra.

"None of that," Nurse Allen says, and I realize I must be crying because she presses a tissue into my hand. I'm still dabbing at my eyes when she says, "Well here's Mr. Prince now."

He's standing in the doorway. A cup of coffee shakes in his hand so violently that Nurse Allen steps forward to grab it and spare the floor.

"I'll give you two a moment," she says, stepping out of the room.

Trap closes the distance to the bed before the door is shut. His arms fold around me like he's terrified he'll break me. "Oh my fucking God," he says smoothing down my hair. "I thought… I didn't know… I wasn't… Oh my fucking God…"

Wires trail from beneath the hospital gown I'm wearing, and electrodes pull at my skin. A plastic cap shifts on my finger, one of those readers that's supposed to monitor my oxygen. Graphs leap on the screen next to the bed.

"I'm sorry," I say, and I'm crying again. "I'm so, so sorry."

"I told you a long time ago, you never need to tell me that," he whispers against my hair. "But sweet fucking Christ, what were you thinking?"

"I don't know. I thought… I wanted… I was so scared…" I'm no better at getting out a sentence than he was, and for a long time, we simply hold each other.

But I owe him more than that. I force myself to sit back, to take a deep breath and say, "Leo bought the Crash from an orderly at—"

"I tracked the fucker down. The jizzstain was fired before your fever broke."

That's such a Trap response I have to laugh. But not for long, because I still have to make him understand. "When I found the Crash in Swallowtail, Leo and I fought. He said—"

"I don't give a flying fuck what Leo said."

And that is also classic Trap. And he's right. This isn't really about Leo. It's about me. About us.

I find his hands. I squeeze them between mine, ignoring the pinch of the oxygen meter.

Words.

I'm supposed to use words.

I force myself to say something I should have managed long ago, "I took the Crash because I wanted to understand Leo."

"Fucking—"

"But I kept taking it because it let me forget. I didn't have to think about… This thing we have… You and me… The stuff we do… I love it. I love you. But sometimes my brain gets scrambled."

"Scrambled how?"

I try a dozen sentences inside my head. None of them fits. None of them is right.

"How?" he asks again. "Just tell me what you're thinking. It doesn't have to be fucking perfect."

"I'm a whore!"

He's shocked. Whatever he thought I was going to say, that isn't it.

I hurry, before I lose my nerve. "You give me everything—a house and clothes and food. Trips to New York. An entire library of books. Anything I want, you're handing it over before I even know how to ask."

"But I—"

"No." I cut him off. "Let me finish. It's not just *things*. It's lawyers. It's a job. It's taking in Leo—"

"I don't—"

"Please! Let me say this. You were willing to take out Jonas and Ansel because of what they did to me. You *know* what it means to kill a man. You've seen what it did to me. But you're willing to kill *two*, because they hurt me. Because they might hurt me more in the future."

His throat works. He wants to interrupt. But he squares his shoulders and clenches his jaw and lets me go on.

"And the only thing I can give you in return is sex. Here. In New York. Inside your freaking car… I'm a real-life, flesh-and-blood blow-up doll."

The shock on his face is the only thing that gives me the courage to continue.

"Sex. Where you want it. How you want it. I'm your whore."

He pulls back. Edges away. I'm going to lose him, but I have to say the last bit. I'm so close to the end.

"I always knew good girls say no. I knew I'd go to school, get good grades, work in a psych lab for the rest of my life. I'd marry another grad student. Maybe we'd have sex on my birthday. On his. On our anniversary. Maybe even once a week, like clockwork, whether we wanted it or not."

Trap doesn't want to hear about grad students, about my having sex with anyone but him. So I clutch his hands. I look into his eyes. And tell him the rest of it, the worst of it, the end.

"But every time we fuck, you and me, I feel things I never imagined. I love being your toy. I love how you know exactly how much I can stand. I love that eternity before you say the word, before you let me come. I'll do anything for that feeling. I'm embarrassed, and I'm sad, and I'm disappointed that I don't have a single shred of self-respect. But none of that changes one basic fact: I'm your whore."

I'm shaking. My head feels like it's floating above my body, attached by a single knotted string. I'm breathing like a racehorse who's just broken a record at the Kentucky Derby.

Trap waits. And waits. And waits some more.

Finally he says, "Can I say something now?"

I nod.

"You're not my whore. You've never been my whore. You're the one woman I've ever loved, the only person I want to spend the rest of my life with. If Nurse What's-her-name walked through that door this minute and told me I could never touch you again, I'd still stay here with you. If Dr. Hanson said you were off-limits for any reason, in any way, I'd sit here till my balls turn blue and fall off, pick them up and throw them away, but I wouldn't leave your side. If you decide you don't want me, if you can't ever stand the thought of fucking me, I'll spend a hell of a lot more time exhausting myself in the gym downstairs, but I'm never letting you go. Not now. Not tomorrow. Not ever."

I open my mouth, not sure what I'm going to say, but he shakes his head fiercely.

"No. I let you talk. Now you have to listen to me. I brought you home from Debasement because I thought you were hot. I had no idea you could tame the Beast. But when I'm with you, the animal in my brain goes to sleep. When I'm with you, that fucker doesn't stand a chance."

"That's because—"

"I'm not done," he snaps. "Because it's not just me you help. It's not just me you heal. You walk around the freeport like you're carrying a goddamn magic wand. You solve problems before I even know they exist. You came up with the idea for the Diamond Ring before you had the first clue about what we really do here. You kept the security guards from walking off the job. You ran the Monet auction like you were born with a gavel in your hand."

I start to deflect his praise. Those things weren't magic. They were examples of applied psychology, of my using years of education to achieve simple, practical goals.

But he cuts me off again. "I swear to God, woman, I'll gag you if I have to."

I have the immediate urge to speak again, just to make him

follow through on his promise. Before I get the chance, though, he says, "Four months. You've been here four fucking months. But it already seems like four years, maybe even longer. I can't imagine running the freeport without you by my side."

I open my mouth. Close it. He's surprised me. Truly shocked me.

"You can't be serious," I finally say, and I rush on before he can cut me off because what I have to tell him is too important. "I'm a liability, not an asset. When we sat in Carver's office, and I blackmailed him without blinking… I'm as bad as Herzog ever dreamed of being. Worse, because I acted on sheer impulse. Weaponizing power is so deep a part of me that I do it without conscious thought."

"Watching you go after Carver was when I realized I can't run the freeport without you. When I knew I needed you to be my Chief Operations Officer."

"You can't be—"

"Say you'll take the job."

His gaze is so intense it feels like a spear, lodging deep inside my heart.

"Say yes," he commands.

"Yes."

"You'll take the job."

"I'll take the job."

"And say you'll never leave me."

"I'll never leave you."

"There," he says, like he just won an argument. And then he shifts our hands, bringing mine close to his chest. "You *are* a good girl. You're *my* good girl. You're my princess. And I should have said this before, should have made this official a long time ago. I should have asked you to—"

The bedroom door opens and Nurse Allen appears with a smile. "Okay, Mr. Prince. Ms. Key. Time for a little rest now."

"We just need a couple of minutes," Trap says, his gaze not leaving mine.

"And you'll get them," Nurse Allen counters. "Right after Ms. Key takes a nap."

The only other person in the world who handles Trap so efficiently is Susan Richards. And thinking about that makes me realize Susan must have had her hands full these past ten days. I can't imagine that anything about the freeport has gone smoothly, with Trap sitting here beside me.

I've made a mess of so many things.

I start to beg Nurse Allen for a reprieve, if only to let Trap finish that one tantalizing sentence. But when I open my mouth to speak, I yawn.

"There," Nurse Allen says. "You see? It's time for a nap, and then you two can have a few more minutes to talk."

She ushers Trap into the hall and closes the door before either of us can protest. And my eyes are closed before she's back by the bed, straightening my sheets and adjusting a couple of wires. I'm asleep before she's taken her seat near the bed.

36

TRAP

I almost lost her.

And Jesus Christ, I don't know if I can take another threat like that. I don't know if I can stand the fear that she'll be taken away. That I'll never see the real Alix again.

Which is why I need to get my hands on Jonas and Ansel Herzog. We're playing a game of cat and mouse, and I'm ready to bring in a fucking Doberman.

Every minute those monsters stay alive, Alix is under threat. That's why I've told Best to use any means necessary to eliminate the brothers. That's why I'm staying in the freeport, taking advantage of *my* fucking fortress. That's why we're at the endgame: It's them or me.

And I've got a reason to win. I've got Alix.

It's easy, the first five days after Dr. Hanson declares her clean. Alix's body is still recovering from the heavy doses she ramped up to in such a short time and from her rapid detox. She sleeps most of the time. I follow the doctor's orders, making sure she eats three meals a day, lots of Vitamin B12, heavy on the fruits and vegetables, tons of protein—all of it good for repairing damaged nerves.

Just like I promised, I keep my fucking hands to myself. My hands, my cock, the tools in the dresser drawer. There's a part of me that wants sex with Alix, that craves that physical bond. But the doctor said Alix needs to heal.

I haven't taken this many cold showers since I was sixteen years old. At this rate, my right hand is going to have callouses an inch thick. The worst part is waking in the middle of the night and knowing she's just inches away. The smell of her… the heat of her…

A sane man would go sleep in the guest room. But I'm never putting that distance between us again.

Of course, none of this can go on forever.

We're sitting at the counter in the kitchen. We watched the sun set over the treeline an hour or two ago. We made a dinner of cheese, crackers, and leftover steak from the fridge. I'm sipping an eighteen-year-old Glenfiddich that tastes like smoke and apples. She's got an over-size mug of chamomile that she's sweetened with honey. The room smells like autumn.

"With everything that's happened," she says, "I almost lost track that Thursday is Thanksgiving. I'm going to see if I can get a reservation somewhere in town."

I frown. "Let's get something catered. I don't want to deal with families and screaming kids."

She nods, like that makes sense. A minute or two later, she says, "There's an auction coming up at Sotheby's. Last one of the year—some really interesting works by Italian Impressionist painters. I thought we could go up there together."

"The timing doesn't work for me," I say automatically. I realize she didn't give me a date and I bite back a wince, hoping she won't notice.

Her eyebrows peak, though. She knows *something's* up. "I

want to go to Tiffany's," she says. "To check out some holiday gifts for staff."

I scowl. "Narrow things down online, and we can have someone bring samples here."

Fuck. I answered too fast. She counters: "I've never seen the holiday show at Radio City Music Hall."

I look her right in the eye and say, "Maybe next year."

"Then how about the National Gallery of Art, down in DC? There's a photography show that just got a great review in the *Post.*"

"No."

She spreads her palms flat on the counter. I watch her take a deep breath. She doesn't count out loud, but she might as well. I can hear the numbers in my own head. When she speaks, her voice is very small. "Is this because I vetoed all your ideas when I was high? Are you punishing me for using Crash?"

"No!" How the fuck can she think that? I reach out and turn her chair, framing her knees with my legs. "It's not punishment. It's common sense. I'm keeping us safe."

"We can't stay locked up here forever."

"We don't have to. Just until those cocksuckers are nailed."

"What if that doesn't happen?" From the way her voice slides into a new octave, I know she's terrified.

I set my palms against her cheeks. "We'll get them. They breathe and eat and shit like everybody else. And they can't keep their heads down forever. We know every home they own. They've got a business to run. At some point, they'll poke their heads over the goddamn horizon, and we'll blow their motherfucking brains out. You just have to wait a little while longer."

She draws a shaky breath, but before she can say anything the wall of glass beside us shatters into a million pieces.

37

ALIX

Trap reacts before I do. He pulls me off the bar stool, folding his arms around me like his body is made of steel. Somehow, he yanks us over the center island, sending the cheese plate flying. I'm fighting him by reflex, struggling to gain my feet, but he drags us down behind the counter. His palm spreads over my head as he presses me into the floor.

Only then do I realize my ears are ringing in the aftermath of some loud sound. My arms are etched with dozens of tiny cuts, each one beginning to ooze a little snake of blood. Cold air rushes in through the gap that used to be windows.

Trap raises a finger to his lips, telling me to be quiet. I obey, because I can't think of what to say. None of this makes any sense.

Trap takes his phone out of his front right pocket. He pulls up the app that controls the smart house—the door locks and the temperature control and the lights. He smashes his finger down on an icon, and we're plunged into darkness.

This can't be happening. We're safe in our own home. How many times has Trap told me no one can see us from the back of the house? How many times has he said the property is secure?

The sound of a shotgun being racked is like something out of a movie. But this isn't pretend. This is our lives.

"Make it easy, Prince," says a voice that haunts my nightmares. "Stand up and take this like a man."

Jonas Herzog.

I don't need overhead lights to picture his muscle-bound chest, his neck like a tree trunk, his arms swollen from hours at the gym. The sound of his voice craters my belly. My throat is coated with burning acid.

Trap turns to steel. He doesn't make a sound, but I can hear him swearing in my head.

I'm not surprised when Ansel's voice rings out, lower than Jonas's. Darker. "He's not a man. He's a pussy."

And Jonas: "We both know what to do with pussy."

Their cruel laughter knifes between my legs. I can picture their cold, cold eyes, the blue of skim milk, as they plot new ways to draw my blood.

Trap's grip on my arm keeps me down. He lowers his mouth to my ear. "Upstairs," he whispers, so softly I need to guess the word. "Gun safe."

He still holds my biceps, keeping me from moving, but I nod. He raises his free hand; I can barely see its outline in the glow from the stovetop clock. Five fingers. He folds one down. Four. I take a deep breath. Three. My legs tense. Two. He releases my arm, and I bite my lip.

One.

With one hand, Trap sweeps a glass from the floor beside us, sending it skittering toward the garage door. At the same time, he shoves me away from his body, away from the kitchen, away from the immediate threat.

I run for the second floor blindly.

I know this house. I've lived here for over five months. I dreamed of it every night I lived in Herzog's cage.

But I'm only halfway to the steps when I hear Jonas's command. "Stop, bitch. Or I'll blow his fucking head off."

Even as I turn back, Trap shouts, "Run, Alix!"

But his words are strangled. I have to stop. I have to look. I have to see by the blue-gray lights of the stove that Trap is pinned against the refrigerator, the barrel of a shotgun pressed across his throat. Ansel is leaning in with all his weight, and whatever else Trap intends to shout is reduced to a hideous gurgle.

Ansel brings his knee up hard, catching Trap in the groin. Then he bashes the stock of the gun against Trap's right temple. Trap slides down the metal door, puddling on the floor like a man with no bones.

Ansel kicks him in the ribs, twice, with booted toes. Trap doesn't stir, which terrifies me more than the look on Ansel's face. How hard was that blow to his head? Oh my God, is Trap even breathing?

I've waited too long. Like a mouse charmed by a cobra, I've let Jonas get within range. His hand on my wrist is an anchor, and he drags me into the dining room like a leaking sack of cement.

Moonlight glistens on the table. The windows look out on the peaceful backyard, an empty stretch of grass that has always felt like safety. Now, it's a moat, an uncrossable stretch I could never conquer even if I managed to break free.

I need to fight. That's what Trap would want me to do. That's the only way I'm getting out of this alive.

But Jonas's eyes shine white in the darkness. He clicks his tongue against the roof of his mouth. Just like that, my mind fogs, like a television with ad reception. Pee dribbles down my leg, and I know I'm going to die.

"Stupid cunt," he says, pushing me into the armchair at the

head of the table. I want to resist, but I can't. I've lost the will to fight.

And then, over his shoulder, he growls, "Get over here, dickhead. Make yourself useful, or I'll cut off your prick and use it to fuck your eyeholes."

He's not talking to Ansel, not with that tone, not with those words. I look past him to the great jagged hole that was the wall of kitchen windows. If there's another person here, I can beg him. I can offer him any amount of money. I can promise him the world, if he'll help me break free.

My heart shatters.

Leo stands in the doorway that leads to the kitchen.

My brother is gaping like a freshly landed fish. The moonlight catches the scars on his head, the places his hair hasn't grown back in. With his broken nose, he looks like a ruined statue.

"Asswipe!" Jonas barks. "Move it!"

Leo crosses the room like a zombie. He takes the plastic zipties Jonas throws on the table. He fastens my wrists to the arms of the chair. He ties my ankles to the legs.

I can't fight. I can't move. I can't believe my brother is working with these demons again. I don't know how he got them into the freeport, but Leo is the reason Trap and I will die tonight.

Jonas digs deep in a pocket and drops something else on the table. "Get that on her," he snaps.

It's an O-ring gag.

I don't know if it's the one Herzog used in his study. I don't know if it's the one that cut into my lips when the brothers took turns fucking my mouth. I don't know if it's the one that gave them free access to my tongue, so they could dose me with Crash the first time.

All I know is it will kill me to wear it.

"Please," I beg. I don't bother talking to Leo. He's just a tool, a machine. He can't decide to save me. I thrust my appeal at

Jonas. "Please," I say again. "Not the gag. Let me suck you off. I promise I'll make you feel good."

"Oh I'll feel good, you fucking whore. When my cock rips your ass in two, I'll feel like a fucking king."

"If you put that on me, I won't be able to beg," I say. "You want to hear me beg, right?"

"I'll settle for you screaming," Jonas sneers. And then, to Leo: "Get it on her. Now."

"Please," I whisper to my brother. "Don't do this. You're a good man. You don't have to listen to them. You don't have to do what they—"

He lashes the buckle so tight, I see stars.

Jonas laughs as he steps toward the kitchen door. "Any time today, moron," he says to his brother.

Ansel shuffles into the dining room with a sheaf of zip-ties in one hand and the shotgun in the other. "I doubled up on him," he says, tossing the plastic ties onto the table. "Don't want the bastard getting loose."

That means Trap is still alive. I need to fight. I need to find a way to survive.

"Not dressed like a kitten tonight," Jonas says to me. And then, to Ansel, "Let's cut her out of this shit."

Ansel parks the gun on the table before he produces a sleek metal capsule from his pocket. I can barely see its shape in the darkness, but his thumb shifts, and a wicked triangle of blade snicks into place. "I've got first dibs," he says. And he grabs the hem of my T-shirt, holding the fabric taut as he uses the box cutter to slice from my neck to my waist.

"First isn't always best, little brother." Jonas holds out his hand for the knife. He goes after the sturdy fabric of my sports bra.

I tug at the arms of the chair. I try to kick my way free. I twist my body, doubling over, doing anything I can to protect my breasts. And all the while, I scream an endless wail, because the gag has stolen all my words.

Jonas fights back. He plants an elbow in the hollow of my throat, making me choke for air. He lands a punch to my solar plexus. But even gasping, I continue to thrash, because whatever he's planning is worse than not being able to breathe.

He catches my hair in his fist, yanking my head against his heaving belly to bare my throat to the ceiling. The box cutter hovers over the stretched line of my jaw. "I'll do it, bitch. I'll cut your throat the same way you cut Klaus. Ear to ear, and then I'll fuck your bleeding windpipe."

There's a strangled noise that I think I've pushed past the gag, but then I realize it's Leo. I can just see him out of the corner of my eye. Tears stream down his face, and he's gasping for air.

But he isn't doing a thing to stop the men who want to kill me.

I collapse back in the armchair. Jonas finishes cutting off my bra. He traces the tip of the knife around my nipples, whispering, "You won't bleed out, if I just take these. We can play for hours."

But Ansel elbows in for his turn. He takes the blade back. He chokes when he realizes my yoga pants are soaked with piss, but he wipes his hand on my bare chest and saws away at the fabric. He yanks the ruined cloth from under my ass and rubs my face with it, like a man teaching a puppy not to piddle.

Jonas grabs back the knife. "Here," he says, thrusting the blade toward Leo. "You get her panties."

I howl in protest. Leo freezes.

Jonas says to my brother, "You cut them off, or I will. And if I do it, you'll eat them. Every fucking bite."

Leo takes the knife.

His hand shakes like he's detoxing from heroin, meth, and Crash all at once. He whispers, "Sorry, Al," but he doesn't meet my gaze. Instead, he slips his fingers beneath the waist band of my plain cotton underwear, gathering it at the side, like this isn't totally, irrevocably depraved.

My brother cuts off my panties, first the right side, then the left. He slides them out from under me and hands them to Jonas, his entire arm juddering like he's at the epicenter of an earthquake.

Jonas crams the cloth against Leo's nose. "Take a deep breath, dickhead. That's your sister's cunt you're smelling. Piss and cream, because she's sick enough to want you fucking her with your shriveled cock."

I'm dry as a bone between my legs, but Leo looks like he's going to puke. Ansel's laughing like a wild dog.

Jonas crosses to the sideboard. He yanks the top drawer hard enough to send silverware flying. I flinch in reflex, but he takes his time searching the debris on the floor.

He comes up with a steak knife in his hand.

"Is this the one?" he asks. "Is this the knife you used to kill my brother?"

I shake my head hard enough to make my spine crackle. He moves the blade closer to my face, pressing the flat against my cheek. I freeze, and the point settles less than an inch from my eye. "I could scoop this out now, bitch. You only need one to watch everything we have planned."

He lowers the knife to the gag, to the tender edges of my mouth that are already torn and raw. "Or we could give you a smile no one will ever forget."

He traces down my throat, edging the knife against my right breast. "My brother gave you these tits. We can take them back. One cut here. Another one there. And you can drink the fucking implants after you stop screaming."

He'll do it. I know he will. My body is trembling so hard the zip-ties are slicing into my flesh. Bright red blood rushes into the creases of my bonds.

But Jonas isn't through. He trails the knife down my ribs. He slides the flat over my mound. He rests the tip at the V where my clit hides. "Cut this out," he says, "and you'll never come again." He tilts his wrist. Points lower. "Or I can fuck you with the knife, bitch. Fuck you hard. Fuck your slit. Fuck your ass. Fuck you till there's nothing left but meat, like you left my brother. I can fuck you to death."

Drool dribbles past my lips. I try to form words, try to make him understand. He can do whatever he wants with his cock. Put it up my ass. Shove it in my pussy. Double up with Ansel, add Leo if that's what he needs, whatever will make us even, whatever will make us right. Just please, please, please put the knife away. Please don't fuck me with the knife.

But I can't say the words. I can't get them past the gag.

Ansel pushes his way forward. He's been busy while Jonas has been torturing me. His clothes are gone; he's naked as an egg from head to toe. He's raided the silverware on the floor too, and his left fist is clutched around a second steak knife. His right hand strokes his enormous erection.

"Let me play, too!" he says, sounding exactly like a child begging to be included in a game of Monopoly.

Monopoly.

Leo and I played Monopoly. I was always the dog, and he was always the racecar, and we paid out double if we landed on Go.

I stretch my neck, looking for my brother. I'll beg him. I'll plead. If he won't save me, can't save me, at least he can pick up his own steak knife. He can make his own cut, a clean one, running from my right ear to my left. He can find my carotid. It isn't hard. I found Herzog's, with one desperate blow.

Leo can still save me.

But he's crouching in the corner. He's twisting a scrap of fabric between his fingers. I don't think he even remembers those are my panties. He's covering his head with both forearms, and he's sobbing into his knees, and I know he'll never set me free.

"Let me play!" Ansel whines again. He jostles Jonas for position. He levels his knife in front of my splayed legs.

I close my eyes and pray to die.

38

TRAP

~

They're gone.

My wrists and ankles are bound tight enough that my fingers and toes are numb, but the cocksucking jizzstain shit-fuckers left without blowing my brains out. I take a deep breath in relief and nearly start coughing at the pain in my side. It feels like they ran over me with an eighteen-wheeler.

I wince, and the skin by my eyes pulls tight. There's something wrong there too, something swollen. A slow, steady ache pounds in time with my pulse. At least that means my heart is still beating.

Shit. My ears are working too.

One of those cumwipes is talking. And when I'm finally able to concentrate on the words, I realize he's torturing Alix, cutting off her fucking clothes.

I can't stand. I can't even sit. I can't rip my hands free from these goddamn ties, even though I try and lose a layer of skin.

Think, asshole. Just think.

But my brain is locked twenty years in the past, and I'm trapped in a metal hut, where I know I'll die if I step over the chalked line around me. I can taste the reeking bodies at the back of my throat, and sweat breaks out of every pore like I really am in Kenya and the blood beneath the zip-ties might already be infected with Ebola.

The Beast detonates inside my skull.

That Herzog bastard had his hands all over me. His fingers were on my wrists. He leaned against me with his full body weight, doing his best to crush my throat with the barrel of his fucking gun.

I'm filthy and I'm doomed and the flesh is going to rot off my bones if I don't find a way to bleed off the Beast *now*. I clench my fists, but that isn't enough. I hit my head against the base of the refrigerator, but the animal inside me won't give up. I tense every muscle in my body—seize, release, seize, release—five times until my ribs are screaming and my swollen eye is bursting and every nerve in my body is on fire.

The Beast reluctantly accepts my offering. It retreats. For now.

Panting, I lie on the floor and try to recover. But my heavy breathing isn't enough to mask the animals in the dining room. They're telling Leo to do something. Fucking Leo Key.

My shoulder is pressing into something hard, something that hurts. It takes me longer than it should to realize I'm lying on a corner of the cheese board. That isn't rocket science. They must have really done a number on my head.

But if the cheese board's here, then the plates are too. And maybe the old-fashioned glass I threw against the wall when I told Alix to get my gun. If the plates or glass broke… If there's an edge sharp enough to cut plastic…

I can't find them, if they're even there. But as I grope across the floor, jackknifing like an electrocuted inchworm, I find something better.

The carving knife. The one I used to slice last night's leftover steak.

Alix is sobbing now, making sounds that don't seem human. They must have her in a gag, an O-ring, the type she hates.

I have to hurry. I can't hurry. If I drop the knife, I may never be able to pick it up again.

I wedge the blade between my hip and the counter. I twist my arms until my shoulders shriek. My bruised—broken?—ribs holler in protest, but I tell them they can shut the fuck up, as I saw my wrists against the blade.

My hands slip, and the knife bites into my skin. *Motherfucker!* Now there's fresh blood in the mix, making everything slippery, a thousand times worse.

Alix moans, and the cumstains in there start to laugh. They're big men, but they're giggling, and I swallow down puke as I shove my wrists against the knife again.

The zip-tie catches. I press hard, ignoring the scream in my shoulders.

The bond breaks.

But it's not the only one. The fuckwits doubled up on me. No wonder my fingers feel like they're made of oak.

Alix screams. She's trying to say words, but I can't make them out. All I hear is pure terror.

I crash my hands down against the knife. I find the second zip-tie. I separate my wrists as much as I can, giving myself the greatest purchase, and I lean my entire body weight against the blade.

My hands pop free.

I feel like I'm wearing mittens, but I scramble for the knife. It takes four tries, but I cut the ties around my ankles.

I pull myself to my feet using the counter. My toes are as numb as my fingers. I feel like I'm stumbling over boulders. But I grip the carving knife and I stagger into the dining room, braced for whatever I find there.

No.

I'm not braced.

I can never be braced for the sight of Jonas Herzog holding a knife between Alix's legs. I can never be braced for Ansel Herzog hunched over the pair of them, his cock bobbing like a deranged seesaw as one hand pumps away like a hundred-horsepower engine. The other grips another blade.

I stumble.

I bay.

I fall against the dining room table, catching the carving knife between my palm and the polished mahogany. I start to pull the blade back, aiming for Ansel's heaving shoulder blades, but then I see a better weapon.

Some part of my screaming brain remembers the sound of the shotgun being racked. All I have to do is pick it up. Brace the stock against my shoulder. Reach for the trigger.

And pull.

39

ALIX

The sound echoes off the dining room walls, filling my ears with a deadening roar. My eyes fly open as I'm caught in a disgusting spray of warm blood and flesh that will haunt my nightmares for years. The room reeks with gunpowder.

The thing that used to be Ansel Herzog collapses at my feet. He falls face down, one hand still gripping his crotch, the other his knife. The space between his shoulders is pulped, a shattered mix of muscle and bone and blood, all black and white in the dim light from the windows.

Trap stands over his kill like a vengeful god. His right eye has swollen closed, and his hands are soaked with red-black blood. He kicks Ansel's naked body, putting all his weight behind the blow.

Ansel's gone. He can't respond. But Jonas does.

Jonas clutches the knife he was scraping against my thigh. He reverses his grip so he can slash with the blade, and he launches himself toward Trap, screaming like a rocket on re-entry.

Trap tries to raise the gun, tries to get off another shot, but Jonas surges past the barrel. There isn't time. There isn't room. Even though he's armed, Trap is at a disadvantage, because his hands are full and the shotgun is suddenly useless.

Not useless. Jonas's knife slides harmlessly off the barrel. Trap is fighting for the distance he needs to set the stock against his shoulder, but he doesn't move with his usual panther-like grace. Instead, his foot slips in Ansel's blood, and he falls hard to one knee.

I catch the glint of moonlight on metal as Jonas tosses away his knife to grapple for the gun. Trap pulls him off his feet, kicking the blade toward the corner. Both men are rolling on the floor when Trap hollers at Leo: "Cut your sister free!"

Leo responds by grabbing his head harder and rocking faster. I can hear his moans over Trap's harsh breathing, even over Jonas's guttural grunts.

"Leo!" Trap bellows like a drill sergeant. "Move your fucking ass!"

Miraculously, Leo moves. He picks up the knife. He crawls toward me. He cringes as Trap and Jonas roll beneath the table. He stares in horror at Ansel's body.

"Leo," I try to say, but the gag turns his name into empty vowels. "Help me. Please."

They aren't real words. But Leo acts. He shakes like a sprung jack-in-the-box, but he slips the tip of the knife under the tie that holds my left wrist. He leans back, using his weight to pop the plastic. Without my prompting, he cuts my right wrist free too. I grab the knife from him and release my feet.

I run for the stairs, stripping off my gag to take deeper breaths. In the dark, the steps are steeper than I remember. I stumble halfway up and have to catch myself on the railing. I bruise my naked hip. But I make it to the bedroom, to the closet, to the gun safe installed inside the wall.

The keypad comes to life when I touch it, gleaming black against green. I know the number. I've always known the number.

I key in zero, six, two, one.

June twenty-first, my birthday. The longest day of the year. The day that changed my life. The day I met Trap.

The safe sighs open. The Sig Sauer waits for me, poised on its rest. My fingers close around the grip like they were forged for this day.

I wheel back to the stairs and the dining room.

Leo crouches by the chair where I was bound. He's fingering the plastic ties, gazing at them like they're jewels from a distant planet.

The shotgun lies shadowed in the doorway that leads to the kitchen. I can't tell if Trap threw it there or if Jonas did, but there's no way either of them can use the weapon now.

Jonas is kneeling on Trap's chest, fingers tight around Trap's throat. Trap is fighting, bucking, but he can't get a purchase on the dining room floor. His face looks like it's turning black, and the sounds coming out of him belong in a slaughterhouse.

I plant my bare feet on the floor. I raise my arms, stiffening both at the elbows to support the pistol. My naked thighs are shaking. My bare breasts heave as I fight to draw a steady breath.

I can't take a shot. The men are too close. They're moving too much. It's too dark, and I'm terrified I'll end up hitting Trap.

"Jonas!" I scream, to draw his attention.

He responds faster than I think is humanly possible. Still keeping his grip on Trap's throat, he pounds Trap's head onto the floor. The wet, meaty sound is drowned out by Jonas's snarl as he staggers to his feet.

Stooping, he snags the knife from Ansel's dead hand.

He whirls toward me as I try to track him with the gun. His face is twisted beyond recognition. He's smeared with blood and worse. He's lunging across the space between us, knife at the ready, hollering an ancient war-cry.

I leap back, but he's moving too fast. I don't have time to aim the gun. I don't have space to twist away. I'm trapped and he's coming and there's no way I can escape…

Leo springs in front of me. Arms wide, chest forward, head back, he puts his body between Jonas Herzog and me.

The knife is silent, sinking home.

Leo's arms wheel, and he collapses to the floor, hands closing over the grip of the blade protruding from his belly. Jonas stares down at his empty fingers, utterly confused.

I raise the gun and fire, a direct hit to Jonas Herzog's face. The back of his head splatters against the dining room wall.

Silence.

But not really. Trap is groaning, rolling over to his stomach, pushing himself up on all fours. I'm keening, my breath moving in and out of a throat so tight it sounds like I'm singing.

And Leo is sobbing.

I limp to his side, taking only a second to place the pistol on the table. Leo's fingers slip on the knife. He's trying to pull it out.

"No," I say, kneeling beside him. Some ancient memory of a first aid class or a Girl Scouts merit badge or maybe just an episode of bad TV warns me that if he moves the blade now, he might bleed out.

I hear Trap behind me. He's coughing, but he's talking into his phone. 911. Emergency.

Leo grabs my hand. "Tell…Alix…I love her," he says between sobs.

"Hush." I try to smooth his hair. "I'm here. I'm Alix."

"No," he protests. "Daughter… Alix."

"Just rest," I tell him. He's not making sense.

His fingers squeeze mine. "Master made me… Gun… Camera… Fuck… Svetlana…."

"Hush," I say, not because I don't believe him, but because I do. Of course Herzog had a gun. Of course Herzog filmed him raping a helpless woman.

Trap is giving our address now. "Just rest," I say to Leo. "Help is on the way."

"Baby… My baby… I get pic— pictures…. If I w— work."

They kept poor Leo in line, kept him chained to a table, just so he could see pictures of his child. He's more agitated now, fighting harder to make sure I believe him. I make soft noises and try to keep him calm. "Shhh," I say. "You can tell me more later."

He shakes his head. He doesn't believe in later. Urgency pushes out four full sentences. "I left here. I needed Crash. I needed Alix. I called the Herzogs."

Tears stream down his face. His teeth chatter so hard, I can barely make out what he's saying. "Please," I say, twisting my fingers around his. "Just wait. You can tell me the rest tomorrow."

"I k— kept ID," he said, defiance making his voice stronger. "For f— front gate. H— Herzogs in trunk."

Trap is talking to the security guards at the freeport gate now. He's telling them to let the police in, to send up the ambulance. He's telling them to hurry.

"H— had to," Leo sobs. "F— For Alix. They said… They said… They…"

It's too terrible, what Jonas and Ansel said they would do to a defenseless child. "They can't hurt her anymore," I say.

"T— tell Alix…"

"I will."

"I l— l— l..."

"You love her, I know."

"You. I l— l— love…"

I'm sobbing too. "I love you too."

He squeezes my fingers with all the strength of a ghost. He slips his hand from mine. He knocks his knuckles against the knife's grip.

He dies.

40

TRAP

I drape a blanket over Alix's shoulders as the red and blue lights pull up to the house. She doesn't seem to remember what to do with it, so I pull it close under her chin. I help her over to one of the dining room chairs and make sure she's covered after she sits.

Before I open the front door, I tap my phone, turning the goddamn lights back on.

My head is pounding, and I can't see out of my right eye, and there isn't an inch of my body that isn't bruised. I'm bleeding from where the zip ties cut into my wrists and ankles, and from the long, shallow gash where the carving knife slipped. My clothes are torn, and one shoe is missing, and my ears are still muffled from the echo of gunshot.

But I'm the person in the best shape, among all of us.

Ansel Herzog is dead, his naked back flayed by my shotgun blast.

Jonas Herzog is dead, half his head blown off from Alix's shot.

Leo Key is dead, a knife still buried in his gut.

Alix is cut and bruised and shaking like a newborn fawn, as naked as the day she and her fucking brother were born. She's staring at the chair where they tied her, eyes unfocused on the dark stain on the seat, and I'm willing to bet she doesn't smell her piss, or the Herzogs' shit, or any of the salt-copper blood that floods the fucking room.

When she killed Klaus, there was no question we would cover up the crime. She wasn't going to pay a price for executing the shitbag who did his best to destroy her.

Tonight is different.

Tonight the bad guys came after us.

They gave us everything they had, tried every move they knew. In the end, it wasn't enough, because Alix Fucking Key is the strongest woman I've ever met in my life.

We're not hiding from the cops tonight.

Tonight we tell the fucking truth.

41

ALIX

My face is pale in the bathroom mirror, washed out against my black sheath dress. My lipstick looks harsh, like I'm a little girl who got into her mother's cosmetics. I wipe it off with a tissue and sigh.

"You look beautiful," Trap says, coming up behind me.

I lean back against him, letting his dark suit frame me. His arms around me feel like home.

His cracked ribs are healed now. His swollen eye has long-since gone down. For both of us, our bruises have faded. Our scabs are gone. Gone, but not forgotten. Never, ever forgotten.

"We've waited a month to bury him," I say. "Maybe we should just forget the whole thing."

"If that's what you want to do." Trap says it easily. Automatically. He really *is* giving me the option.

But as Dr. Martinelli has pointed out more than once in our therapy sessions, my life has been suspended these four weeks.

I've run on auto-pilot, dealing with lawyers and with the police. I've accepted the daily crop of paparazzi at the front gate. My greatest accomplishments have been signing off on work orders for the house, approving the installation of new windows in the kitchen, and authorizing a complete gutting and renovation of the dining room.

This time, no one found any hidden surveillance equipment.

Dr. Martinelli is right. She usually is, on the rare occasions she makes definitive statements. Mostly, she asks questions and waits for me to reply. That's what a good therapist does.

Trap is waiting. If I give him the word, he'll call off the minister, tell the funeral home to store the casket a while longer, order the cemetery to pitch a tent over the gaping hole in the ground, or fill it back in, or whatever else I desire.

"Let's finish this," I say.

"Good girl," Trap says. I remember when those words used to kindle something inside me. Not now. Maybe never again.

He kisses the top of my head, and we head outside to where our driver waits with the Mercedes. Charles has more patience than I ever would, edging forward at a few miles an hour to keep from crushing any of the camera-toting fiends outside the freeport gates.

"Fucking parasites," Trap mutters.

"Will this *ever* end?"

"Today should be the last of it. You'll make your statement, and there won't be any more life in the story."

"My statement!" I've forgotten the notes we prepared so carefully.

Trap pats the breast pocket of his jacket. "I've got them right here."

Of course he does. He has everything I need. He always has. Always will.

His fingers wrap around mine lightly. I lean back against the leather headrest. My eyes are closed when I ask, "Do you think we should have looked harder?"

"For Alix?"

It still feels strange, hearing my name refer to someone else, but I nod. "She should be here."

"She's three years old," he says. "No three-year-old would understand her father's funeral."

If she even exists.

He doesn't say that part out loud. We've debated it too many times over the past month.

Trap has paid Harry Asher an ungodly amount of money to track down Leo's daughter, without a single hint of a whisper of a possibility of a solid lead. We started with my brother's cell phone. I was able to get into it easily enough, using the four-number password Leo always used—the number of the house where we lived when Mom was still alive, before Dad married Candace, when everything was perfect.

That got us access to his contacts—none. And his emails—none. The entire phone was locked down, stripped of apps, managed with the strictest possible parental controls.

Leo communicated with one person: Jonas Herzog. Texts arrived at irregular intervals, starting November 30, the first year I was held in the New Castle house.

JONAS

Finish the shipment by midnight tonight and you'll get a special reward

On December 2, Leo wrote back.

LEO

Bring her back to the warehouse

JONAS

If you pack enough this month

LEO

She's MY daughter

You can't do this

Please

Just send a picture

The communication was silent for nearly six weeks, and then Jonas finally responded.

JONAS

Hard work earns rewards

He attached a photo of an infant. The baby had dark hair. She was sleeping, swaddled in a pink blanket. Her mouth was pursed in a tiny rosebud. Her impossibly small fingers curled around a necklace with a gold-painted charm, a Russian icon. Black letters were only visible when the picture was expanded: Saint Svetlana.

The communication continued irregularly. Jonas issued demands for more work, for faster work, for fewer hours of sleep. Sometimes, he provided pictures of the baby. A lot of the time, he didn't.

Intermittent reinforcement, my psychology training supplied. The subject does not receive reinforcement each time they perform a desired behavior; instead, rewards are random. Subjects consistently yield the greatest effort, study after study after study.

Leo was turned into a lab rat. A Crash-packing, slave-bound lab rat.

Cole Wolf analyzed every pixel for us. The photos are real. The child really exists. But there's no way to say that she's Leo's daughter, my niece.

I still doubt myself enough to say to Trap now, "Maybe I missed something in Herzog's records."

"You didn't."

"You can't know that."

"I know you went through those files like your own life depended on it." His voice stays absolutely even as he recites the facts we've both memorized. "You found Svetlana's purchase order. You found her bill of sale. She was shipped to Abu Dhabi a month after she arrived at the New Castle house."

I found the video too, the one that haunted my brother. I only watched it once, but that was enough. Leo was in an all-too-familiar room, Klaus Herzog's study. He was fellated by a man, both of them terrified, Leo barely responding. Ursula led in a frantic woman who begged in a language I was pretty sure was Russian. Leo raped the girl.

Even if he impregnated her, she probably wouldn't have known when she was shipped to the United Arab Emirates. After her sale was final, there was no reason for the Herzogs to track her. Her new owner could have kept her, could have killed her, could have done anything he wanted with the baby, if it ever existed.

The photos sent by Jonas to Leo are just another cruel blackmail—like the video of me killing Klaus, like the recording of Bart Carver raping me, like Leo with Svetlana. That's how the Herzogs work. That what they do.

Worked. Did.

We arrive at the cemetery. There's no reason to do this in a church—Leo didn't believe in God. He never mastered Narcotics Anonymous' second step: "We came to believe that a Power greater than ourselves could restore us to sanity."

God and I aren't on speaking terms either. I'm still half-convinced I'm actually living in hell. That's why men like the Herzogs exist. That's why women like me are tortured.

But living in hell doesn't account for Trap. It doesn't explain the man who helps me out of the car. Who walks me to the small dais set up at the cemetery gates. Who stands beside me as the paparazzi swarm like maddened hornets.

He reaches into his jacket and passes me a folded sheet of paper. He hands me a handkerchief too and waits for me to dab beneath my eyes. He glares at the cameras and murmurs, too soft for them to hear, "You've got this, Princess."

I clear my throat and shift the angle of the microphone. I glance at the paper, but I don't actually need it. I've memorized the words.

"I'll make this statement, but I won't take any questions. Travis Prince and I are here today to bury my brother, Leo Aidan Key. Rumors have spread that Leo and I were estranged, but we reconciled before his death. My brother gave his life to save me when Travis and I were attacked in a brutal home invasion. The murderers who destroyed our peace were inflamed by the sort of photos and videos you people peddle as cheap entertainment. Their deaths and my brother's death now put an end to this tragic chapter. There's no further story. Nothing else to see. We hope that you will all do the honorable thing now and move on. Let us grieve in peace."

A few of the paps call out questions, but their cries die off like echoes in a mine. Trap helps me down from the platform. The cemetery gates are already open, and we pass through like we're entering our own private kingdom.

I take Trap's arm as we walk the cobbled path to the gravesite. We're the only mourners at this sad little ceremony. I phoned my father and left him a message, asking if he would come. He had his secretary reply that he'd be out of the country. I hadn't even given him a date.

The minister meets us with a somber nod. He opens his book, but he seems to know his lines as well as I knew mine at the gate. The words are familiar from movies and TV shows. Ashes to ashes. Dust to dust.

Silent cemetery workers lower the casket. I drop a clod of earth onto the wood. Trap does too.

I've never been a fan of burials. Personally, I want to be cremated. But I want there to be a marker for Leo. Somewhere my father can visit, if he ever chooses to forgive. A place for little Alix to see, if she actually exists.

The walk seems shorter, heading back to the cemetery gates. Someone has cleared away the little dais and the microphone. Charles is waiting with the Mercedes, the door already open. The paparazzi are gone.

42

TRAP

I can make sure the refrigerator is full of all the foods she loves—hand-picked berries in the middle of winter and ten different kinds of olives and cheeses with names I can't begin to pronounce.

I can keep the heat at seventy-seven, five degrees higher than I'd leave it if I lived alone.

I can subscribe to a dozen magazines and leave them around the house, ones with pretty pictures, with engaging articles, with cartoons I'll never understand.

I can wait.

Because the one fucking thing I can't do is get inside Alix's brain. I can't force her to feel safe. I can't make her believe that none of this—not one goddamn second of it—has ever been her fault.

Dr. Martinelli helps. Maybe it's because of Alix's background in psychology. Maybe it's because the shrink came recommended by Dr. Hanson, who already gained Alix's trust.

But Alix has gone from three sessions a week to two, and she's talking about dropping back to one.

It's only been a month. That's nothing, compared to all the time she spent in Herzog's house. It's a blink of an eye, compared to growing up with Leo.

Fucking Leo. Every time I picture his goddamn face, I want to break the shitbird's nose again. I never should have let him on freeport property. Never should have trusted him.

And when I threw his ass out, I should have made sure he didn't have his fucking freeport ID in his pocket. That's on me. I didn't frisk the cocksucker. And I didn't think to cancel his access after he was gone.

The cumstain was a miserable excuse for a human being. He was broken. Utterly destroyed. It never occurred to me he'd have the balls to take any initiative, much less to open the door to the motherfucking Herzogs.

I flip off my reflection in the bedroom window, both middle fingers stiff. This has become my own nightly ritual—turn the lights on, stand in front of the glass, look out at the darkness, and tell the world to go to fucking hell.

We should have been safe here. They never should have gotten to us.

I've ordered the fence raised around the perimeter another five feet, and an all-new laser system will detect anything larger than a robin. I've doubled security staffing throughout the freeport and added two dozen cameras. I've hired bodyguards for Alix and me; they're stationed in front of the house 24/7.

But not the back yard. I won't give in on that. I built this house so I could look out at those trees and know I'm the one in fucking charge.

If Alix asked, though, I'd turn off the bedroom lights. If that's what she needed to feel safe, I'd plunge us both into darkness. If that was the price for taking her to bed, I wouldn't hesitate a second.

She can't do it. Not yet. I don't know if she'll ever be able to.

I hear her come out of the bathroom. I smell the mint of her toothpaste. I watch her in the glass, see her sit on the edge of the bed, take hand lotion out of her nightstand drawer and massage it into her fingers.

"Hey," she says after a century or two, which I've spent telling my brain to cool it with the fucking memories of how she feels beneath me, how she sounds, how she tastes.

"Hey," I say back, turning toward her with a smile that feels like it's cracking my jaw. Fuck me. She's wearing her terry robe. It's tied tight around her waist. It rides up on her hips where she's crossed her legs. Her toenails are painted the same shade of pink as her lips.

She unties the robe and slides it off her shoulders.

She's wearing satin and lace, black with strategically placed crimson bows that make me hard before I can swallow. The bra's the one she wore at the train station. It barely covers her incredible tits. The bows on the panties rise and fall with her breathing, so fast a sane man would offer her a paper bag to keep her from hyperventilating.

I'm not sane.

I have other ideas for helping her to calm down. Filthy ideas. Ideas I have no right to ask for.

"You don't have to do this," I say. "If it's too soon… If you're not ready…"

"Do I look not ready to you?"

"You look fucking incredible."

"Prove it."

I cross the room and reach for the lamp on her nightstand. If she truly means to give me this gift, I'll make it as easy for her as I can. We can fuck in the dark.

She catches my wrist with cool, calm fingers. "Leave it," she says.

I sit beside her on the edge of the mattress. I cup her face in my palm as I say, "I love you."

She leans into my hand, just a little. "I love you too."

Jesus fucking Christ. I'm supposed to be an expert at this. I'm supposed to know exactly what to do, how to turn her on, when to snap an order that'll bring her to her knees.

But I don't want to break her. I don't want to take more than she can give.

"I'm not made of glass," she says, because after everything we've been through, she can read my fucking mind.

"I just want to be sure—"

"Red means stop," she says. "Yellow means slow down. Green means go. Go hard. Go very, very hard."

She's learned her lessons better than I ever could have dreamed when I picked her up at Debasement. Her lips are as red as the strawberries I fed her that night. Her eyes are still the same whiskey brown.

"All right, Princess," I say, purposely making my tone hard. I'm rewarded by a flare of hunger across her face. I point to the bottom dresser drawer. "Leather cuffs," I command. "Hands and feet. Hurry."

She jumps like a greyhound out of the gate. While she's digging for the tools, I toss her robe toward the wall. My shirt follows; I pull it over my head, not wasting time with the buttons. I've got my belt undone and my fly unzipped when she comes back with the bonds.

She kneels in front of me. Like a goddamn dream, she sinks to her knees, bowing her head like she can't see the massive hard-on two feet from her lips.

Her tits are straining that bra like they're desperate to be free. Only a superhuman could keep from reaching down and twitching the black hooks apart.

I'm not a goddamn superhuman.

I'm a man. And I groan when the silk slips away, revealing nipples so hard they're a fucking invitation to be sucked.

If I do that, I'll blow my load faster than a fifteen-year-old boy in the back of his father's Chevrolet. So I do the next best thing. "Suck them," I tell her. "Left one first. Suck it hard."

She hated those tits when she came back to me. But I remember the first night I had her in this room. Her nips were so sensitive that a pinch between my fingers was enough to make her safeword. These new ones aren't so fucking tender. These new ones open up whole new worlds of possibility.

She clutches her tit with her left hand. Bends her head. Pulls the nipple into her mouth, sucking hard enough to hollow her cheeks.

My cock gets so hard I have to shift my feet to keep my balance.

I drop my pants to the floor, then my boxers, kicking both away. I fist my dick, the same move I've used for the past four weeks to find a hint of relief.

But this is different. This is watching Alix. This is listening to the wet, sloppy sound of her pleasure. This is stroking once, holding it, going back to the root and pulling again, long and slow, the way I'm going to fuck her hot, sweet snatch.

Her right hand slips inside her panties. The back of her wrist presses against silk and lace, finding an angle that lets her fingers plunge deep. Without my permission, she stops sucking. She throws her head back and arches her neck, pinching her wet nipple hard with her left hand as her right fucks her pussy.

"Stop!" I command, because rules are rules. Because I'm the one who tells her what to do. Because if those plump lips don't close around my cock in the next seven seconds I'm going to die.

She stops, because that's her choice. She stops because she wants to. She stops because that's the way we play in this room—me in control of the tools and the game, she in control of her safeword.

"Did I give you permission to touch your cunt?"

She doesn't like the word. I see that on her face. But she shakes her head and answers honestly. "No."

"Then what should be your punishment?" I ask.

And she says the words I've been dying to hear. "Whatever you command."

I command her to get off her fucking knees. I command her to lose the goddamn panties. I command her to let me smell them, let me breathe in deep as she gets on her back in the middle of the bed.

I snap my fingers for her left wrist, and she complies. I make the leather cuff tight. Secure. When I lash it to the bed, she moans.

I snap for her right wrist. Make her give me one foot, then the other. She's spread on my bed, mine to control, the shallow bowl of her belly trembling as she waits.

Her pussy looks like a goddamn flower.

I climb onto the mattress and kneel between her legs. She's freshly shaved, her skin smooth and clean. I don't need that anymore; the Beast is long-since silent where Alix is concerned.

But I like it. I like it a lot. I trace my thumb from her navel to her clit, watching her wriggle at the promise.

One tap to that hard button, short and sharp, and she leaps from the bed like I fired off a shot. Her knees try to close by reflex, but she's tied too tight for that.

She can't escape as I work her with my fingers, stroking, gliding, then coming back with harsh, hard taps. Her hips rise to meet me. Her hands clench on the straps that bind her to the bed. She points her feet, stretching, reaching, because it's been a goddamn month for her too, and she needs me as much as I need her.

I climb off the bed.

She makes a surprised sound, something between a moan and a groan and a question. She opens her eyes. She waits.

She waits, because that's another part of our game. When she lost her mind on Leo's fucking stash, she finished without my permission. I'm jealous that she came. I hate that she didn't need me.

And to prove to her that she needs me now, that I need her, that we need each other like a fucking forest fire needs oxygen, I stalk over to my jeans and whip my belt from the denim loops.

I've beaten her ass with my belt before. I've made her wear one like a collar. But now I climb back in the bed and I fist the leather, leaving a length half as long as my cock.

I slap her clit with the long flat tongue, hard enough to make her gasp. She doesn't shout a warning, though, doesn't give me yellow or red. So I land another blow, steady and hard and perfectly on target.

"Please…" she begs, and she's so fucking close it's a crime not to send her.

But I'm a criminal mastermind when it comes to Alix. I land the belt again. Again. One more time—perfect placement—and her clit glows red and her pussy opens and she's poised for everything I can give her.

I rock back on my heels.

"Please," she begs. "Just say it. Just tell me. Let me come."

"Not yet, Princess."

"I'll do anything you want. I'll suck your cock. You can fuck my tits. You can pound my pussy. You can't be too rough."

"My sweet, good girl. That mouth on you. You've learned everything I ever wanted to teach you."

She must remember as clearly as I do, the way she lay in this bed without words to describe her own body. She couldn't say what she wanted. Couldn't tell me what she needed. But she listened, and she learned, and now she'll be mine forever.

She's fighting the leather cuffs, trying to break free. I don't know if she wants to get her hands on my cock, or if she wants to fuck that hot ready pussy with her own desperate fingers, but it doesn't matter. She's not getting away.

"Please," she whispers. "Please, please, please."

And because I love her, I bury my face between her thighs. I suck on her clit, as hard as she pulled on her own nipple. I lap at the honey that pools beneath that pearl. I thrust my tongue deep, feeling her melt against my chin, my nose, my entire greedy face.

She's on the edge. She's suspended on a wire. A woman who didn't have her iron will would have fallen by now.

But she's my princess. She's my good girl. She holds herself tight and waits for my command.

It's almost as bad for me as it is for her when I push back from my feast. Worse, maybe, because my cock is made of fucking granite.

"Trap," she whispers, and I love the sound of my name on her lips. "Say it."

"Not yet."

"I'll do whatever you want."

"I know."

"You can fuck me up the ass."

I freeze.

She doesn't mean it. That's her one hard limit. The one thing she's never allowed.

"Trap?" And now my name is a question. "I mean it. My ass is yours."

I tried, the first night I had her. The Beast had its claws deep in my brain. It said I couldn't fuck her if her ass wasn't plugged.

But Alix, my sweet Alix, broke at the touch of hard, black rubber. She panicked. She shouted *red* loud enough to shatter stone.

Now I say, "You don't have to do that." The words are as rough as a cat's tongue.

I never forced her, but Herzog did. All three brothers took her up the ass. They made her take their cocks, and when that didn't satisfy the sick, twisted perverts, they forced other things up her hole.

"Trap," she says, and her saying my name pulls me back from my rage. "I know I don't have to. But I want to. I want that from you."

I meet her eyes. My hands fall to my sides. I say, "Red means stop."

"And yellow means slow down," she says, her voice steady and clear. "And green means go. Please. Go. Green."

I sink back between her thighs. My lips find her clit for another long kiss. My tongue traces her sweet slit.

And then I slip lower. I find her tight little pucker. I lick it, soft at first, like she's melting ice cream, and then hard, like she's a ring of solid sugar.

Her thighs are tight. She isn't talking now, isn't moving. She's in her head, which isn't where I want her to be.

I reach up and find her clit with my fingers. I tap a rhythm that I match with my tongue—tap and swipe, tap and swipe—steady, even, predictable.

She's primed. I did that without knowing how we'd play this out. Her clit swells beneath my fingers. Her hips tilt.

"Trap…" she whispers, and this time I answer her.

"Come," I say, my lips almost touching her perfect rosebud. And as she breaks, I push my tongue into her, breaking past her tightest band, reaching the dark, soft heat beyond.

43

ALIX

Trap's fingers are warm and hard, framing my clit. His thumb is in my pussy. His tongue is inside my back hole, thrusting deep as I clench and clench around it.

It's filthy and it's nasty and it's wrong in so many ways, but the vibrations rolling through my body say otherwise. As I crest, I call on that god I don't believe in, worshipping and praying as the thunder goes on and on.

Trap rides with me, shifting his hands so he frames my hips. He pulls me closer to his devilish mouth, rising only once to repeat his command.

"Come," he says again, and I do a second time while he kisses my pucker and licks me and tells me that I'm beautiful.

When I'm done, when I've crashed back to earth, when I can open my eyes and raise my head and wonder what I did to deserve this incredible man, he rocks back on his heels.

He reaches for my left ankle first, undoing the leather bond.

He unties my right ankle. He climbs off the bed and frees my wrists, right, then left.

I move slowly, lowering my arms. I feel the delicious stretch of what we've done, and I know my sides will ache tomorrow. I flex my feet. I slowly raise my knees.

And Trap leans over from the side of the bed. He scoops me up like I weigh no more than a kitten. He pulls me to the edge of the mattress and flips me over, waiting for my feet to find the ground before he levers his weight against my back.

He has me pinned against the bed, my feet on the floor, my arms caught beside me as my belly and breasts and head are supported by the sheets. He straddles my back and bends down close to my ear.

"One more time, Princess? Can you do that for me?"

I'm his princess. I'm his very good girl. I can feel his cock, heavy against the small of my back, and I know I'll do anything he asks of me.

"Yes," I say. "For you."

He kisses my ear. My neck. And he rises off me, leaving me aching with a whole new kind of loss. I close my eyes because I never want to be alone like this again.

I hear the door of my nightstand slide open. A rustling as he reaches for what he wants. A funny sound, a slurping sound that would have embarrassed me before Trap knew all my secrets.

His lube-filled palm slides along the cleft of my bottom.

Another slurp. I hear his breath catch and I know him well enough that I can picture the iron line of his jaw. I know what his cock looks like, sliding beneath his hand. I can picture the glisten of lube.

His hands are slick on my wrists. He pulls my fingers from my sides. Places them on my bottom. Tightens over them, and I realize what he wants me to do.

I want to do it too.

I pull at my butt, spreading and separating. I offer myself to him without hesitation. Without reservation.

He anchors one hand on the small of my back. With the other, he brings his cock to my tight back opening. He pauses for just long enough that I could shout a color if I wanted.

And then he slides home.

It hurts. His magnificent cock is huge, and my body tenses in reflex.

But he goes slowly, giving me time to relax. He's in perfect control. His palm is light on my back now and my own hands slip to the bed.

And as I yield to him, as I give him this the way I've given him every other part of my body, he fills me. His chest presses against my back. His hands frame my shoulders. His belly tenses.

And when he starts to move, my world transforms.

I thought I knew my limits. I thought this would hurt me, but it was something that he wanted, something I could give him when he's given me so much. I thought I could close my eyes and I could bear it, because I've borne so much already.

I was wrong.

I was wrong, because this is like nothing I've ever experienced before.

I crave surrendering to Trap. My body and my mind—they need to be dominated by him. In the safety that he's built for me, I've learned to hand over control in exchange for utter satisfaction.

But nothing about sex with Trap has prepared me for this intensity. Not his toys, not our games, not any of the things we've ever done together. My nerves are super-charged, delivering a thousand times the sensation they've ever carried before.

"Sweet fucking Christ," Trap groans. I laugh because it's so perfect, because Trap is riding me, with his foul mouth and his beautiful cock and his perfect understanding of my body.

My laughter frees something in him. I didn't realize he was holding back; I didn't know he was still afraid of hurting me.

But he grits out, "You like that, Princess?"

"Yes," I sigh.

"You want it rough?"

"From you."

"You want it hard?"

"Always."

He's pumping now, fingers digging into my hips. I know that grip. I'll have bruises in the morning.

I push back into him, wanting even more.

He slaps my ass, and just like that I'm on the edge of an orgasm. My fingers tighten on the sheet. My neck arches.

I match him on his next thrust, whining with need.

"That's it, Princess," he says. "Show me you can take it. Tell me that you want it."

"I can," I gasp. "I do."

He's close to the edge himself. His breath is roaring now. His hands are iron clamps, binding us together.

"Please…" I beg, because that's what I do with him. For him.

"Come," he orders.

He isn't touching my clit. His fingers are nowhere near my pussy. But as he delivers his command he releases into me, hot, hard pulses that shatter my nerves, stretching me and spinning me and pulling me under and I'm coming harder than I've ever come in my life.

I can't see.

I can't breathe.

I can't stop.

When my brain begins to stir again, I realize I'm kneeling beside the bed. My cheek rests on the mattress. My thighs are shaking so hard I wonder if I'll ever stand again.

Trap sits beside me, leaning his back against the bed. He pulls me onto his lap, holding me as I shiver. The furnace of his body warms me, calms me, soothes me back to something human.

"My good girl," he whispers against my hair. "My sweet, good girl."

He has a warm washcloth, and he wipes between my legs, long soft strokes that melt my mind. I must drift off again, because I wake on the bed. Trap's sitting behind me, his legs a V of safety around mine.

He holds a glass to my lips, and I swallow the most amazing drink ever invented—ice-cold water. He smooths my hair from my forehead and tells me I'm magnificent, and then he feeds me chocolate.

I want to tell him I'm all right. I want to tell him he's amazing. I want to say we'll be together forever and ever and ever, but all those words are too complex.

"I love you," I whisper, because it's simple. Because it's true. Because it will be true forever.

"I love you, too," he says, and I fall asleep with his arms around me.

44

TRAP

She looks so vulnerable in the twilight, like she's made of china or seashells. But that's not right, because china and seashells are hard and brittle; they break under the slightest pressure.

Alix is tough.

Alix is strong.

Alix can kick my ass six ways to Sunday, even if I used her so hard last night that we both slept the entire day.

She's earned her sleep. That's why I slide out from under the covers, doing everything I can to make sure I don't wake her. Downstairs, in my office, I find a series of emails from Susan.

She's drawn up an itinerary, with entries on every quarter hour. She's confirmed my flight plan, with ground transportation on the other end, along with restaurants and hotels. She's listed contact information for a dozen different people if anything goes wrong.

The last email is a blank message, but the subject line reads: Good Luck.

Smiling like a fucking idiot, I head back upstairs.

I shower in the guest bath. Creep into my closet and pull on clothes—my black jeans will do, with a matching T-shirt. It's December, so I add a sweater, the black one with a snag in the right shoulder.

It's time to wake Alix. She'll need a little time to pack.

In my absence, she's rolled over onto her stomach. Her legs are tangled in the sheets, giving me a glimpse of her amazing ass.

This evening's trip was planned long before last night. This isn't a trade-off. It's not payment for services rendered. What I have planned has nothing to do with the gift she gave me last night.

Gift… That hot, tight channel…

I drag my fucking mind out of the gutter. Her trust. I mean her trust. She knows I'll never hurt her—at least, not in any way she doesn't jones for.

I lean over and bite her on the ass.

"Trap!" she says, jerking awake.

"Rise and shine, Princess."

She groans. My cock stirs, ever hopeful, but it's not that type of groan. "What time is it?"

"Almost six."

Another moan of despair. "In the morning?"

"Evening. You slept all day. We both did."

"Then there's no reason not to go back to bed right now."

I laugh, because I don't think she realizes how much that sounds like an invitation. "Hey, Chief Operations Officer. I'm not the one who thought the freeport needed a conference on cybersecurity and museums."

"Fuck…" she mutters. I try not to preen at the positive effect I've had on her. "Forget about the conference," she says. "I'll look up some articles on Google."

"And pass up the chance to see Paris?" I yank the sheets to the foot of the bed. "We've got exactly three hours before wheels up at the airfield."

I expect her to hustle. Instead, she strikes a pose, looking like one of those women in the paintings she loves so much. "It's your plane, right?" she drawls. "You can pay the pilot overtime to wait."

The temptation is strong, especially when she looks up at me through her lashes. But I'm able to keep my eyes on the prize. "Not tonight, Princess."

She pouts, which really is almost enough to make me give in. Instead, I walk to the bedroom door. "Three hours," I say. "They're holding dinner on the plane."

I go wait in my office, because I'm a fucking genius who knows the goddamn limit of his ability to resist temptation.

45

ALIX

I blink as we circle the Arc de Triomphe, our driver threading his way through a dozen lanes of traffic like a jockey at the Kentucky Derby. On the plane, I made Trap take his pillow and his blanket to his own bed, so we're both surprisingly awake in the bright morning air of Paris. There's a lot to be said for private jets.

But even a billionaire can't clear away traffic in a major European city. I glance at my phone. "We're going to be late," I say.

"Relax."

"You know what's guaranteed to keep a woman from relaxing? Someone telling her to relax."

"You want a guarantee on relaxation? I have an idea or two that might work."

I blush.

After everything Trap and I have done together, after all the things that have happened in and out of the bedroom, he still has the ability to make that swoop ripple through my belly, to make color rush to my cheeks.

He laughs as the driver works his way across another massive traffic circle, this one with an obelisk in the middle. I can see the Seine out my window and a dusty little park beneath winter-bare trees.

The driver pulls over to the curb.

"Where are we?" I ask. "This isn't the conference center."

"I want to make a quick stop."

"Trap!" I protest. "The keynote speaker is one of the world experts on—"

"Humor me," he says. He leans across me and opens my door, gesturing for me to step out of the car.

The December sun is brilliant, but a sharp breeze cuts across the plaza. I pull my coat closer around my shoulders, hoping Trap's quick stop doesn't involve public exposure in a Parisian park. He leans back into the car and says something to the driver who gives a friendly nod.

As the car drives away, Trap slips a hand under my elbow. I can't believe he's only wearing a sweater in this weather.

"Let's go, Princess," he says.

He leads the way to a low stone building. The long side of it is lined with windows that overlook the river. I can glimpse potted trees inside, their greenery broken up by oranges.

Trap leads me to the front entrance. It looks like a Greek temple, complete with columns. As we approach, someone pushes the door open from the inside.

"Monsieur Prince," says the man, softening Trap's last name with his heavy French accent. "I hope your trip was easy."

"Yes, thank you," Trap says as we pass inside.

"*Très bien*," the man responds. "Very good." He leads us through a metal detector, but no one seems to be on duty. "If you would be so good as to follow me…"

I glance around, trying not to look like a lost American tourist. I'm sure that I fail, because that's exactly what I am—a lost American tourist who's late to the meeting she signed up for months ago. An information desk sits unattended, but there are slots for pamphlets in French and English. *Musée de l'Orangerie* says one, the letters stark against a brightly colored background.

I know about the Orangerie. I've read about it in books. I've seen its collection reproduced and read essays about the works that line its walls.

"Trap," I say. "What are we doing here?"

He just smiles. Our guide gestures to the far end of the empty lobby. "You'll want to start your visit in the Petite Rotonde," he says. And when we reach the door, he says, "Please. Let me know if there is anything I can do to help you enjoy your visit."

"Thank you," Trap says. "We definitely will."

Our guide disappears through a door that says, in English and French, *Authorized Personnel Only.*

I hesitate outside the entrance to the Petite Rotonde. "What's going on?" I ask Trap. "Where is everyone?"

"Enjoying a well-earned day off," Trap says. "Well, the people who work here, anyway. Tourists who want to visit? They'll have to come back tomorrow."

"Trap!" I say, because the grin on his face is outrageous. Because no one should have that type of power. Because I'm grateful beyond words for the opportunity to see some of the world's greatest artwork without fighting through crowds.

"Ready?" he asks.

"Ready," I confirm.

And he leads me through the Petite Rotonde into heaven.

The room stretches out like a football field. It's shaped like an oval and painted white, floor to ceiling. A massive skylight stretches overhead.

The walls are filled with four gigantic paintings by Monet. They're water lilies, purple and green and brilliant. They're taller than I am, curving with the space. It's like standing in the middle of a garden, like breathing in the middle of a painting, like moving through a brilliant, sun-struck dream.

And it's ours to look at. Ours to breathe in. Ours to absorb without needing to jostle strangers, without needing to wait our turn, without needing to use imagination to fill in the spaces blacked out by others' bodies. I turn around slowly, utterly, completely awe-struck.

And when I turn back, Trap is kneeling on the floor in front of me.

He's taken off his sweater. He's wearing his black jeans and a T-shirt that shows the ripple of every one of his muscles. That's how I first saw him, outside a Dover bar, Debasement. That's how he looked the night I dared to go home with him. The night I became his for the first time. The night he became mine.

He reaches for my hand, holding it fast between both of his. I start to tremble like sunlight on the waterlilies around us.

"Alix," he says, but his throat is tight, and he has to clear it, which makes my heart stutter into triple time. "Alix," he says again. "The night I met you, I never imagined what you would mean to me. I just thought we'd have a good time. I thought you'd be out of my life the very next day."

Bound, gagged, and gone by dawn, that's what he told me that night in the bar.

"I never should have left," I whisper.

"I never should have let you go."

He didn't. I sneaked out. And he spent thousands of dollars and countless hours trying to find me.

"I've lost you too many times," he says. "I don't like the man I am when you're not with me. You're the one who slays the Beast. I can't stand to live when you're not around."

"I'm not going anywhere," I say, my words so soft they're almost lost in the paintings.

"Will you marry me?"

He reaches into his pocket and pulls out a blue velvet bag.

It's cinched at the top with a crimson ribbon. He works the binding, opening the mouth, and he tips a rock onto his palm.

It's the size of a grape, gray with lots of broken edges, almost a sphere. It looks like something a child would find on a playground.

"It's a rough diamond," he says. "The last from the ones my father gave me."

The ones that saved his life. The ones he carried out of a stinking house of death. The ones that built the freeport.

It's priceless.

"Let me make you a ring, Alix. Say you'll stay forever. Marry me."

I don't know when I started crying. I'm not making a sound, but my tears are hot on my cheeks. I want to say I don't deserve this. I want to tell him I'm not right.

But he knows exactly who I am. He knows the woman he brought home from Debasement, the one too shy to ever dream of asking for what she needs. He knows the woman who murdered a man in his dining room. He knows the woman who went back to her darkest nightmare, who tried to drag him down amid the muck. He knows the woman who nearly lost herself to an angel who was never really there.

He knows me.

He knows me, and he's kept me, and I'll be his forever.

"Yes," I say. "Oh my God, yes."

He stands then. He pulls me so close I can feel his heartbeat through his T-shirt. He spreads one hand on the back of my head, and the other on the small of my back, and he kisses me so long, so hard, so deep that I'm drowning among the waterlilies.

"Princess…" he finally says.

I don't have any words. But he holds me until I stop shaking. He laughs when I ask to hold the rock. He waits till I stop crying.

And then he says, "So teach me. Tell me about these paintings. That is, if you don't mind missing the conference on cybersecurity."

"Who cares about a fucking conference?" I ask.

And he laughs as I start to tell him about the art.

I hope you enjoyed reading *Priceless Diamond.* We're just getting started with Diamond Ring romances! Next up is an Irish Mob retelling of Jane Eyre, the true love story of Braiden Kelly and Samantha Mott.

Buy *Irish Brute* Now!
https://alixkey.com/PB4US

BONUS SCENE

~

You just read how Trap gave me a rough diamond when he proposed to me. Want to see what happened when that diamond was turned into an engagement ring?

Get your bonus scene by typing:

https://alixkey.com/Bonus3

into your phone or computer browser.

MORE DIAMOND RING

One last thing: If you want an absolutely free full-length, totally stand-alone Diamond Ring novel, featuring a gender-switch Jack and the Beanstalk retelling and starring Irish mobster Connor Boyle, I've got you covered! Just type:

https://alixkey.com/sins

into your phone or computer browser.

THANK YOU

I can't thank you enough for choosing *Priceless Diamond* from among all the dark romances out there! Without readers like you, I would never have my writing career.

You may not realize it, but *you* can be my hero. Study after study shows that the number one reason a person reads a book is because that book was recommended by a friend.

So will you tell one friend about *Priceless Diamond*?

Of course, if you're dead-set on reviewing my book on Amazon and Goodreads, I won't complain! Honest reviews are hugely helpful because many advertisers require me to have a certain number of reviews before I can buy ads.

Leave a review on Amazon
https://alixkey.com/KI3US

Leave a review on Goodreads
https://alixkey.com/GR3

Whatever you do, don't be a stranger! I look forward to hearing from you soon!

www.alixkey.com
alix@alixkey.com

ABOUT THE AUTHOR

Alix Key was born in Potomac, Maryland, where she grew up making her twin brother and all her dolls act out her favorite fairytales. When an all-grown-up Alix discovered that very real dangers lurk in the woods, she figured out how to rescue herself. She now lives outside Dover, Delaware with her own Prince Charming. When not writing dark romance, Alix serves as the Chief Operations Officer of Diamond Freeport.

You can learn more about Alix at her website, www.alixkey.com.

www.ingramcontent.com/pod-product-compliance
Lightning Source LLC
LaVergne TN
LVHW091115080826
845145LV00008B/1928

* 9 7 8 1 9 5 0 1 8 4 7 6 7 *